On His Majesty's Service

Dedication:
For Cathie, Diane and Georgia

For information on other Trailblazer
books, see our web page
www.christianfocus.com

On His Majesty's Service

Helen Roseveare

Irene Howat

CHRISTIAN FOCUS

Helen Roseveare: On His Majesty's Service
© Copyright 2007

ISBN: 978-1-84550-259-1

Published by Christian Focus Publications Ltd,
Geanies House, Fearn, Tain, Ross-shire
IV20 1TW, Scotland, UK.
Tel: 01862 871011
Fax: 01862 871699
www.christianfocus.com
email: info@christianfocus.com

Cover design by
Daniel van Straaten

Printed and bound in Denmark by
Nørhaven Paperback A/S

Contents

Piggy in the Middle

Helen ran into the house from the garden when she heard her mother calling her name, only taking time to do three cartwheels on the way.

'I know what Mother's wanting,' she grinned. 'Our new nursemaid is coming this afternoon and she'll want to tell us all the usual stuff about behaving.'

Bob, Helen's older brother, was already sitting beside Mrs Roseveare when the girl crashed into the room. Their little sister, Jean, was on her knee.

'Really, Helen,' said her mother, 'when are you going to develop some ladylike behaviour? Your entrance was more like a young pony cantering into its stable than a girl coming into a sitting room.'

Winking at his sister, Bob decided to delay the inevitable.

'I think Mother's right,' he said. 'You are like a pony.'

Helen, who loved her brother and tried very hard to please him, knew exactly what he was up to.

'Ponies are lovely!' she laughed. 'I don't mind a bit being told I'm like a pony.'

'That's all very well,' Mother said, shaking her head. 'But the fact is that you are a girl and doors should be opened and gone through rather than treated as hurdles in a field.'

'I would love to have a pony!' said the girl eagerly.

But she was just a fraction too eager, and Mrs Roseveare suddenly realised that her clever children were up to their usual tricks. They were trying to keep her off the subject of new nursemaids and how not to behave when they came.

Bob and Helen knew they had gone a little too far a little too fast, and they settled down to 'the talk.'

'Now,' said Mother seriously. 'You can be the most delightful children, but sometimes – just sometimes – you forget yourselves and become little demons. My problem is that you often forget yourselves when a new nursemaid comes, with the result that she has hardly unpacked her bags before she starts packing them up again. This really will not do.'

Helen and Bob hung their heads.

'When your new nursemaid arrives this afternoon I want you to behave perfectly. Show her what delightful children you can be … then keep it up. And whatever you do, don't play your awful tricks on her. Do you hear me?'

They heard.

* * *

'Children!' Mrs Roseveare's voice called out to the garden a few hours later.

The two youngsters answered straight away. They walked across the grass together and went quietly into the house where they were introduced to the young woman who had come to look after them.

'You must be Bob,' the nursemaid said, holding out her hand.

Bob shook it politely then took a step back.

'So you must be Helen.'

The girl held out her hand and allowed it to be shaken.

'I'm looking forward to getting to know you,' the nursemaid told her young charges.

Mrs Roseveare decided that the introduction had gone well enough and should not be prolonged.

'Out you go and play,' she told the children.

Bob and Helen nearly forgot their manners when they were let loose, but remembered just in time.

'Walk across the grass until we can't be seen,' Bob whispered.

And that's what they did. But as soon as they were out of sight the pair of them fell into fits of giggles.

'Did you like her?' Helen asked.

'She seemed just like all the others,' answered Bob.

'How long do you think she'll stay?' his sister wondered.

Bob laughed aloud as he kicked a chestnut into the air. 'I suppose that rather depends on us. But I don't think she'll last more than a month.'

'A month's a long time if she turns out to be very strict,' worried Helen.

'If she's as strict as that,' her brother said darkly, 'we won't let her last that long.'

* * *

Not many weeks later Mrs Roseveare was once again looking for a new nursemaid, and she was none too pleased about it.

Yet again Bob and Helen were subjected to 'the talk', and this time it was given with great seriousness. Did they not know that they needed a nursemaid to look after them and their little sister, Jean? Did they not know that their parents struggled to find suitable young women? Did they not know that nursemaids cost money? Did they not know that there were many, many children in England in the 1930s who didn't have the privilege of having a nursemaid to look after them? And did they fully understand how disappointed their parents would be if the new nursemaid, who was just about to arrive, was to depart within a few short weeks?

In the face of the facts that were so clearly set out before them, both Bob and Helen had the good grace to feel ashamed. The problem was that baiting nursemaids had become a game with them, one that they enjoyed. The game was won when the young woman in question handed in her notice and began to pack her bags, and they had won every game so far.

But what the two energetic youngsters didn't know was that while they had won each game so far, they were about to lose the match. Enter Freda.

The weeks that followed were interesting. After they had recovered from the lecture they'd received from both their parents, Bob and Helen were up to their tricks once again. At first they just tried little things they thought might frighten or upset Freda. But the young woman, who was all of fourteen years old, was neither easily frightened nor given to being upset. Then the pair of them moved on to more serious tactics, none of which had the least effect on their new nursemaid! Were they losing their touch?

'I really believe that Freda and the children are going to get on,' Mrs Roseveare dared to say after two months had passed. 'The children seem to like her.'

Her husband put down his newspaper and considered the matter.

'You're quite right,' he said. 'We've had no tantrums from either the children or the nursemaid. Perhaps Freda is just who we've been waiting for.'

In the nursery Helen, Jean and Freda were involved in the serious business of making a birthday card for Bob. He had been given something to do in the garden so that the card could be made in secret.

'Can you keep a secret?' Helen asked.

Freda handed her the glue. 'Of course I can,' she replied. 'A nursemaid has to be able to keep secrets.'

'What do you mean?'

'Well,' said Freda, 'if you forget to behave and do something really silly, what should I do about it? Should I rush downstairs and tell your father and mother? Or should I tell you that you've been naughty, punish you, and forget about it?'

Helen's eyes lit up! Suddenly she knew why she and Bob had given up trying to get rid of their nearly-new nursemaid. Freda liked them and she knew how to keep a secret. She didn't tell Mother all the little things they did wrong! And when she punished them for being naughty, she then forgot all about it.

'I'm glad you can keep secrets,' Helen told her. 'May I tell you a secret?'

'Go on,' teased Freda. 'Tell me and see if I can keep it.'

Helen put her arms round Freda - splashing glue on to her apron as she did so - and told her that she liked her very much.

* * *

'Hurry up and get changed for bed,' Freda told the children a few evenings later, 'or your mother will be up before you're ready.'

There was a hurrying and a scurrying as Bob and Helen put on their night clothes and Freda finished bathing their sister.

'I can hear her coming!' giggled Helen, taking a run and a jump for bed.

Mother opened the door and came in smiling, enjoying the good feeling of a happy nursery and a contented nursemaid.

'What have you been doing this evening?' she asked Helen, stroking her long shiny hair.

'I've brushed my hair a hundred times,' the girl said, 'and I've drawn a picture of the dog.'

'May I see it?' asked Mrs Roseveare.

Sitting down together on Helen's bed, mother and daughter looked at the drawing and then both knelt down and prayed. Helen prayed first and then her mother asked the Lord to bless her. As the little girl scrambled into bed she felt a warm glow inside her. Much as she loved Freda, it was very special to have her mother come up every night in order that they could pray together.

When Mother had gone, and Freda had done the last of the night's tidying and closed the bedroom door, there should have been silence and the soft noises of children sleeping. There was not.

'Will you read me a story?' asked a little voice.

That was a request Helen could rarely refuse. 'Come in beside me and cuddle right down under the blankets.'

Instead of two children sleeping soundly, there was a torch-lit huddle as Helen found their place in a story book and began to read.

'Listen,' whispered Helen, 'we're coming to the exciting bit.'

Jean, her little sister, held her breath and waited to hear what would happen next to Peter Rabbit in the dangerous territory of Mr McGregor's garden!

Most nights after she had read her little sister a story, Helen lay for a while and thought. She tried to puzzle out the unfair things in her family life, the kind that happen in every single family. Why was she sometimes punished when she'd not done anything wrong? Why did the others not tell Mother when she was smacked for something they'd done? Why was Bob allowed to do things she couldn't do just because he was two-and-a-half years older? Why was Jean let off with things because she was a year and a half younger? In Helen's opinion being the middle one of three children was the worst thing to be. She wasn't special because she was the oldest, nor was she special because she was the youngest. In fact, she was just the piggy in the middle.

'What would I like most of all?' she sometimes wondered before she nodded off to sleep. In her heart Helen knew the answer. Her dearest wish was to be Bob's favourite sister, to be his very best friend. She worked out ways of pleasing him, games they could play, puzzles they could do. But whatever she did, Helen felt that her sweet little sister was his favourite and that everything she tried always went a little bit wrong. Poor Helen, if only she'd known it, part of the problem was that she tried far too hard.

* * *

'Happy birthday to you. Happy birthday to you. Happy birthday, dear Helen, happy birthday to you!' sang the family after breakfast one Sunday in September 1933.

'Imagine you being eight years old,' smiled Freda. 'I'm quite sure you didn't think I'd still be with you on your eighth birthday!'

By then Freda was so much loved and trusted that Bob and Helen had told her the mischievous things they had done to the nursemaids who had looked after them in the past. Helen opened her little birthday present and just knew this was going to be a good day. Mrs Roseveare took her two older children to church as usual and then they all went home for lunch. Sunday was often the only day her father spent at home and that made it feel special. Her birthday made it extra special.

After lunch the children went to Sunday School, which was held in the teacher's home not far from where the Roseveares lived.

'What are we going to do today?' Bob asked, when they arrived.

The teacher took some papers from her desk.

'I've collected special pictures for you to paste into your Missionary Prayer Books,' she said.

'What's special about them?' asked the birthday girl.

'Look and see.'

Helen looked through the sheets of paper. 'They're all pictures of Indian children,' she said. 'Are we going to make Indian pages in our books?'

'We are indeed,' her teacher agreed.

The afternoon seemed to pass quickly as Helen looked at the different pictures: girls squatting on the ground helping their mothers to cook, boys playing. Then there were pictures of Indian men talking and women carrying loads of wood for their cooking fires.

'Tell me about Indian people,' said Helen, fascinated by the pictures.

'Some of them will have been to church and Sunday School today, just like you,' the Sunday School teacher explained. 'But many, many others have never heard about God.'

'Why not?' Bob asked, looking up from his Missionary Prayer Book.

'They've never heard about God because no-one has ever gone to tell them about him,' he was told. 'Much of India has never been visited by missionaries.'

Helen thought about this and felt sorry for the child whose picture she held in her hand. She looked into the child's dark eyes and tried to imagine what it would feel like never to have heard about God.

'I'm going to be a missionary when I grow up,' she told her teacher. 'That's what I want to be.'

* * *

A few months later Helen was no longer piggy in the middle for she and Bob had another little sister. And, quite amazingly Freda, the nursemaid, was still there!

'Where are we going?' Helen asked her mother as she buttoned up her winter coat.

'I'll explain as we walk,' Mrs Roseveare said, taking her by the hand.

Helen glowed at the thought of having Mother all to herself.

'We're going to church,' her mother explained.

'But it's not Sunday,' Helen puzzled aloud.

Mrs Roseveare smiled. 'I know, but it's still a special day. We're going to thank God for Diana's safe arrival.'

Helen thought of her little sister and smiled. She was very cute, especially when she was asleep.

Helen and her mother were shown into a side chapel of their church in Preston, the north of England town in which they lived at that time. The girl shivered. It was November and very, very cold. Looking round to see who all was there, Helen discovered that it was a private Communion service, and that only the minister taking it and one other man was present. Mother and daughter knelt side by side and Mrs Roseveare pointed to each word in the Prayer Book as it was read or said in order that Helen could follow the service.

'I wonder what that means,' the eight-year-old thought, when her mother's finger paused on the word 'oblation'.

Later, as they walked hand-in-hand on their way home, Helen remembered the word.

'What does oblation mean?' she asked.

Mrs Roseveare's grip tightened and her pace seemed to speed up. Something told the girl that she'd said the wrong thing, or perhaps interrupted her mother's thinking about the service. And a wave of sadness passed through her heart. Here she was having a special time with her mother and she had gone and spoiled it by asking what 'oblation' meant.

'I always spoil things,' she thought. 'I wish I could stop myself doing that. But I don't know how.'

* * *

Between home and church there was a little shop that sold all sorts of curious things.

'I love that shop,' she told Bob one day as they passed on their way to church. Helen ran ahead of the family in order to spend a minute looking in the window before the others caught up and she had to move on.

'Look at those!' she whistled. 'They're beautiful.'

Bob was not convinced that the bookends in the shape of angels were lovely at all!

'Please let nobody buy them,' Helen prayed week

after week, as she saved her pocket money to buy the angels for her mother's birthday. And it was always a great relief to find them still in the window each time she passed.

'How many times are you going to count your money?' Freda asked. 'It's not going to become more just by being counted, you know.'

'I know that,' laughed Helen. 'But I've nearly enough now. Do you think they'll still be there next week?'

Bob was just about to suggest that they would be sold, when Freda caught him with a warning look.

'I dare say they will,' the nursemaid said. 'If they've not sold over all these weeks, I imagine that they'll stay in the window for just a few days more.'

It was a very excited girl who went into the fascinating shop and bought the angel bookends for her mother's birthday, and Mrs Roseveare was pleased when her special day came round and she received them.

* * *

There were very few things Helen enjoyed more than a real rough and tumble game in the garden, the rougher the better.

'What kind of example are you to your little sisters?' Freda laughed. 'Even your brother doesn't get himself into the scrapes you do.'

Helen thought of her sisters – three of them now since the arrival of Frances, the latest and last baby of the family, and felt as though she was a disappointment to them all. She had such a need to be liked, to be best at things, to be able to jump highest, run fastest, shout loudest and be first in the class. The truth is that the only person Helen usually let down was herself because, once again, she tried too hard. She really needed someone to sit her down and explain that she was loved just for being Helen Roseveare, not because of anything she could do or achieve or win. But nobody did.

* * *

'Have you all done your homework?' Helen's teacher asked.

While most heads nodded, one or two children avoided looking at their teacher, a sure sign that their homework was not done well, or even not done at all.

'Right,' the woman said, 'will those on the back row bring their homework to my desk. When I've checked it, the next row can come out. While you are waiting I want you to check through your eleven and twelve times tables ready for a test after playtime.'

There was a very quiet rumble of protest that the teacher decided to ignore.

'Mary,' the woman said crossly, as she looked at one exercise book, 'how often have I told you to wash your hands before doing your homework?'

Mary's head hung low.

'I'm afraid I'll have to write to your mother if you don't do as you are told.'

Mary blushed deeply, mortified at the thought of the letter she might have to carry home to her mother. Not only would she get a row at school, but she'd be smacked at home too!

'Next,' the teacher said.

Helen stepped forward.

'Thank goodness for the Helen Roseveares of this world. At least we don't have eggy mathematics or gravy on grammar from you.'

Helen felt a warm glow inside her as each part of her homework received a red tick.

'Good work!' wrote the teacher at the bottom of the page. 'Keep it up.'

Smiling, Helen picked up her homework book and turned to go back to her desk.

'Next,' said the teacher.

* * *

The warm glow lasted all morning, because Helen not only had all her homework right, she came first in the times tables test, as usual.

'How long did you spend on your twelve times table?' the teacher demanded.

Lucy looked down at her desk. 'Please miss, half an hour.'

'I beg your pardon,' snapped the woman.

'Half an hour,' Lucy said more loudly.

'Well you're going to have to spend much longer than that to get it into that head of yours,' was the thoughtless reply. 'Look at Helen. She said it perfectly, and I'm sure she could have said it perfectly backwards too.'

Helen's warm glow began to fade. Yes, she knew she had said it perfectly. Yes, she probably could say it backwards too, even though she'd never tried that before. But the nine-year-old was honest enough with herself to know that she didn't have to try half as hard as Lucy when it came to mathematics. Working with numbers came quite naturally to her, while poor Lucy spent more time counting her fingers than she did writing the answers when the class did their maths lesson.

As Helen walked home from school that day, she had an honest think about things.

'It's not surprising that I'm good at maths when Father used to be a maths teacher. And he must have been very, very good because he's now an inspector who goes round different schools to see if teachers are doing their work well enough. But I'm not as good as Bob,' she thought. 'He's brilliant! I'm glad he's not in my class at school or I'd never be first!'

The Day Helen
didn't meet Hitler

'This is one of the most special days of my life,' Helen laughed happily.

'Why's that?' Uncle Ray asked. 'It can't just be because you're driving through the Swiss mountains with your godfather in his rather fine car. Can it?'

Helen giggled. 'Kind of,' she said. 'But it's really because it's just nice to have you to myself.'

Driving in the car with her godfather, while her parents travelled in the family car behind them, was a very special treat for Helen.

The girl basked in the comfortable company of her godfather. In fact, she was so relaxed that she told him some of the tricks she and her brother had got up to with the nursemaids who had come and gone before Freda's arrival.

'I don't believe it!' Uncle Ray laughed heartily. 'I knew you were a little monkey, but I would never have guessed at that. Frogs, did you say? Wonderful!'

His laughter was lost in the loud tooting of a car coming from the opposite direction.

'I suppose I'd better move over to the side of the road and let this fellow past,' said Uncle Ray. 'It's one thing playing tricks on nursemaids, it's quite another playing them on car drivers!'

Driving through Switzerland was like a dream for Helen. She loved its beauty, and the flower-filled meadows, the snow-topped mountains and the deep blue Swiss lakes made her feel as though her heart could burst with happiness. And, when she was allowed to drive alone with Uncle Ray, life took on a whole dimension of happiness that she'd never known before. Sitting in the open-topped car, with the wind blowing her long hair behind her, she felt like the queen of all she could see.

* * *

'So tell me what you'd like to do when you grow up,' her godfather asked, as they drove.

Helen had no hesitation about the answer.

'I'm going to be a missionary,' she said. 'And I'm going to go to places where the people have never heard about God and tell them all about him.'

This took Uncle Ray rather by surprise.

'I see,' he said. 'And how do you learn to be a missionary?'

The girl thought for a moment.

'I don't know,' she admitted. 'But I'll ask my Sunday School teacher. She knows all about these things.'

Suddenly her eighth birthday flashed into her mind, and Helen told her godfather about the pictures of Indian children her teacher had collected for them, and how each child in Sunday School had a Missionary Prayer Book full of pictures and maps and facts and figures about mission work.

'Your Sunday School teacher has made quite an impression on you, young lady,' Uncle Ray said thoughtfully. 'I'll look forward to seeing what the future brings and whether you do go abroad one day as a missionary. That would certainly be an interesting life, if a dangerous one for a young woman.'

* * *

Danger was on their minds as the pair of them wove south through the mountains that divided Switzerland from Italy, for they were heading for Campagnia and the ancient city of Pompeii.

'Tell me about the destruction of Pompeii,' said Helen.

Uncle Ray laughed.

'No, you tell me what you know and I'll fill in anything you miss out.'

Helen took a deep breath.

'Well,' she said. 'A young man called Pliny watched what happened from the other side of the Bay of Naples, though it was his mother who first noticed Mount Vesuvius beginning to smoke. The people didn't think it was too dangerous, but early the next morning lava crashed down the mountain at 60 miles an hour and the whole city was buried.'

'I think the only thing you missed out was the date!' Uncle Ray said. 'And that was 79 AD.'

The girl shivered despite the bright sunshine.

'It's terrible when things like that happen,' she said.

'Yes, I've no argument there,' agreed Uncle Ray. 'But somehow it seems even worse when it's people who hurt and kill each other.'

There was a silence as they drove the next few miles.

'Do you think there will be a war?' Helen asked quietly.

War seemed to be what adults talked about most of the time, the possibility of war with Germany.

'I hope not, Helen. And I think our leaders still have time to prevent that happening. If they don't, millions more people will be killed than died in Pompeii all those years ago.'

* * *

Although talk of war continued, when the following summer came round Mr Roseveare thought it was quite safe enough to travel through Europe once again with his wife and three older children. This time they visited Germany, Hungary, Bulgaria and Turkey in their car, with all their camping gear stowed away behind them. The highlight of that holiday was something very special indeed.

'Are we really going to the Olympic Games in Berlin?' Bob asked, hardly able to take it in.

'We are indeed,' said his father.

So it was that in August 1936, Mr and Mrs

Roseveare, along with Bob, Helen and Jean, joined the vast crowd gathered to watch the Games. And when they left Berlin for Hungary, they had plenty to talk about.

'I think it's amazing that a thirteen-year-old girl won a gold medal for diving,' Helen said excitedly.

'You'll have to practise hard if you want to beat her record,' commented her father.

'She can't do that,' Bob pointed out. 'At the time the next Olympic Games she'll be fifteen!'

'What I think will have amazed Chancellor Adolph Hitler is that Jesse Owens, who won four gold medals and broke eleven Olympic records, is a black American,' Mr Roseveare said. 'He seems to think that fair-haired German types are superior in every way to all other peoples.'

Mrs Roseveare agreed. 'It was splendid to see Jesse Owens very publicly befriending Luz Long, his German rival. But I'm afraid Herr Hitler would not have been very pleased about that.'

'Surely black people are just the same inside as white people,' Helen said, though she had seen very few black people in all of her life.

'Of course they are,' her father insisted. 'If they bleed, they both shed the same red blood.'

As they drove from Germany to Hungary, Helen thought of the black athletes she had seen, big strong muscular men and women who could run like the wind.

'Not all Africans are tall and strong,' she remembered from her Sunday School teacher's lessons. 'There are little pygmy people in Central Africa too, but they'll never win a race in the Olympic Games! They might win something else though.'

* * *

'I'm afraid the time is coming for us to leave Preston,' the children were told, not long after they returned home to England.

'Do we have to leave?' Jean asked. 'I like it in Preston, and all my friends live here. I won't know anyone if we move away.'

'Yes, we do have to move,' began Mrs Roseveare. 'Inspectors of Schools are not allowed to stay in the same place for more than three years at a time.'

Jean looked disbelieving. 'Why?' she demanded.

'It's quite simple really,' her mother said. 'Their job is to go round schools checking that teachers are teaching properly and that children are learning all they should. If school inspectors were to stay in one place all of their working lives, they would get to know teachers and headmasters and perhaps not be truly fair in their work. It's just fairer for them to move to different parts of the country.'

'But it's not fair on us,' grumbled Jean.

'It's hard for you,' agreed Mrs Roseveare. 'But I'm afraid that you'll find as you grow up that life is hard sometimes and it's not always fair.'

'The move won't affect me quite so much,' Helen said, when she and Bob were discussing it later. 'I'll be going to boarding school just about the time the family move house. But it's strange to think that when I go home on holidays it won't be to a house that I know.'

'You'll get used to changes,' Bob told her. 'And you'll get used to boarding school too. It's not a bad life really. Have Father and Mother decided where you're going to yet?'

'No,' Helen laughed. 'But they've taken me to visit two and I hope I don't go to either! One was like an army camp and in the other the girls all looked as though they had broomsticks stuck up the backs of their dresses. They stood as rigid as your tin soldiers. And the uniform they were wearing! It was awful!'

* * *

'Wales!' gasped Helen. 'If I go to school in Wales, you'll not understand what I'm saying when I come home on holiday!'

'Don't exaggerate,' her mother scolded. 'We'll be in Kent by then, so your Lancashire accent would be unusual down there anyway.'

But when Helen was taken by her parents to visit the school in North Wales, she knew it was the right place for her. Instead of a uniform dress and straw hat, the girls wore culottes and different coloured cotton shirts. And they didn't look in the least like tin soldiers. Helen began to look forward to boarding school.

* * *

'We're going to have a wonderful holiday this year,' Helen told her little sisters. 'And I'll tell you all about it when we get back. Come and I'll show you in the atlas some of the places we're going to.'

She traced a line from Preston, in the north of England, across the North Sea to Norway.

'We're going to sail in a coastal steamer along some of the Norwegian fjords,' she told them, 'before we travel north right into the Arctic Circle.'

'I thought you were going to Lapland,' said Jean, a little disappointedly.

Helen assured her that they were, and that Lapland was in the Arctic Circle.

'Will you see Father Christmas?' Diana asked.

'I think we're more likely to see reindeer,' said Helen. 'There are thousands of reindeer in Lapland.'

'And then where do you go?' asked Diana.

Tracing her finger south through Finland, Helen pointed to the city of Leningrad (now St Petersburg), which used to be the capital city of Russia.

'It sounds exciting!' said Diana, who liked the thrill of anticipation. 'And when we're older we'll go on foreign holidays too.'

Helen agreed.

So it was that, on a bright summer day in 1937, Helen stood on the deck of a Norwegian coastal steamer in a very uncharacteristic pose. Her mouth was hanging open! She had come on deck as they entered a fjord and her mind could hardly take in the beauty. The fjord was narrow and deep and the mountains seemed to rise from the very sides of the ship. As they reflected in the still water it was difficult to see at first glance where the water ended and the reflection began. Head held back (and, I'm afraid, mouth still hanging open) Helen looked up to the snow-capped mountain tops glistening in the summer sun. Only the loud laughing of gulls brought her out of the trance in which the sheer beauty had placed her, and just for a moment, for even the gulls, swirling and sweeping above her, fitted right into the sheer wonder of it all.

'I'll never see anything more wonderful than this,' eleven-year-old Helen thought to herself. 'Never ever.'

But just a short time later, within the Arctic Circle, Helen was to see another beauty, one so stunning and fantastic that it found a special place in her memory from which nothing could ever steal it, even the most awful things that were to happen to her in the future.

'I think we are going to see the *aurora borealis* this evening,' said Mr Roseveare.

'What's that?' asked Helen.

'It's other name is the Northern Lights,' Bob explained. 'And it's a light that makes strange patterns in the night sky.'

As the family watched, the dark night sky streaked with a strange light that moved and swayed across the heavens. Its colours changed as it wove its wonderful patterns, sometimes bright and shining, sometimes fading into a mere suggestion of itself before jumping into life and streaking across the sky once more.

'It's like a heavenly kaleidoscope!' breathed Helen, in sheer delight.

From time to time, during ordinary days at home, Helen wondered what she should thank God for when it came to her prayer time before going to bed. That night, as she watched the *aurora borealis*, her heart swelled with amazement at God's wonderful world.

'I could stay here forever,' she thought.

But she could not, for Mr Roseveare's well worked out plans meant that they must leave Lapland and travel south through Finland before crossing the border into Russia and their final planned excitement of the holiday. Leningrad!

'I'm looking forward to seeing the bridges,' Bob said. 'There are about 300 bridges in Leningrad, some over the Neva River and the others over the canals that weave through the city.'

'What are you looking forward to?' Mrs Roseveare asked her daughter.

Helen said that what she most wanted to see was the great Winter Palace and Hermitage Museum. But memorable as these were, what stuck in her mind was their train journeys in Russia, for all the trains were guarded by armed soldiers, and all sight-seeing had to be done by government permission. While Bob was fascinated by the weapons the soldiers carried, somehow they almost sent a shiver up Helen's spine.

'I don't like the feeling of being guarded by soldiers,' she thought. 'It's all right if you know they are on your side. But what would it be like it they weren't?'

* * *

When Helen started boarding school everything was new and exciting. Well, sort of exciting. Some things took her a little by surprise. For example, it was strange to go from being a senior girl in a junior school to being a junior girl in a senior school. And because Helen felt she often made a mess of friendships, she was just a little bit scared to make the same mess again. As a result, most of the girls in the new first form found themselves gathering together in groups and Helen felt excluded.

'My dad says that we are going to war with the Germans, and that we'll beat Hitler,' she heard a girl say.

'I was introduced to Hitler at the 1936 Olympic

Games in Berlin,' Helen commented quite quietly. The whole room fell silent and every eye turned in her direction.

'You've met Adolph Hitler?' several girls said in unison. 'I don't believe you.'

'I have,' Helen insisted. 'We were on holiday in Germany that summer and went to the Games. For the first time ever a flaming torch was carried by a relay of runners all the way from Olympia in Greece to the Olympic Stadium. And when the last man ran into the stadium with the flame there was a great cheer. It was just after that I was introduced to Hitler. He was there for the ceremony and so were we.'

All afternoon girls asked Helen question after question about her meeting with Hitler, and by the time she went to bed that night the twelve-year-old could hardly tell truth from lies. Yes, she and Hitler were both in the Olympic Stadium when Fritz Schilgen ran in with the lighted torch. No, she and the German Chancellor had certainly not been introduced. But what did that matter? Not for the first time Helen found that telling lies made her popular, and it felt good to be popular. Sadly, she discovered that popularity built on lies only lasted as long as people believed her, and after that she was less popular than ever.

'Today we are going to do an exercise on simultaneous equations,' the maths teacher told her class. 'Please work out the answers to the problems I've written on the blackboard.'

There was silence for a few minutes as brains and pencils got into gear.

'Yes, Helen,' the teacher asked, noticing that she had finished writing. 'Do you have a question?'

'No, Miss,' said the girl. 'I've finished the exercise.'

'I want you to answer all the questions, not just the first one,' explained the teacher patiently.

'I have done them all, Miss.'

Sighing, the woman asked Helen to take her book out to the front, fully expecting only one or two of the problems to be completed. But they were all done. And they were all correct.

'You like maths?'

'I like it very much,' Helen admitted.

'What other subjects do you enjoy?'

Thinking for a moment, the girl replied, 'I like all my subjects, Miss.'

The teacher smiled. 'You'll be a very popular girl with your teachers then,' she said.

'But not with the girls,' thought Helen sadly. 'The only time girls want to be friendly with a swot is when they can't do their homework and they need some help!'

* * *

There were times when Helen was rather sad at school, especially on those occasions when she got it into her head that she had been sent away to boarding school because her parents didn't want her at home. But deep down she knew in her heart that she was at boarding school because her parents thought that was where she would get the best education. Had Helen been able to read the minds of the girls in her form she might have discovered that many of them had the same doubts when they felt a bit down too. The truth is that the days passed busily and, in the main, happily during the years the teenaged Helen Roseveare was at school in North Wales.

* * *

Helen was not the only member of her family in that part of Britain for, after the outbreak of the Second World War, her father was transferred from the Inspectorate of Schools to the Headquarters of the Ministry of Food. He was known to have a very brilliant mind, and the War Cabinet wanted to use it to help Britain win the war.

'What exactly do you do?' Helen asked her father, when he took her out one Saturday afternoon.

Mr Roseveare thought for a moment before answering. 'You know that all families have ration books because of the war. When they need food or clothes they have to give the shopkeepers tokens from their ration books. This means that poor people get enough, and rich people don't get too much.'

'That seems quite fair,' commented Helen.

'So it is,' her father agreed. 'But what many people don't realise is that this has to be carefully worked out so that people are not being promised food that can't be supplied. For example, if a ship with a cargo of corned beef is crossing the Atlantic Ocean from Argentina to England and it is sunk by the Germans, the Government needs to be able to work out how that will affect the rations people can have.'

A friend of Mr Roseveare, who was spending the afternoon with them, chipped in.

'Your father has an amazing mind,' he said. 'I was in his office with him when a call came from London telling him that a cargo ship had been lost at sea. He sat there in silence for about two minutes and then was able to tell the government official at the other end of the phone the fine details of how the loss of that cargo would affect the country's rations. And he didn't need a paper and pencil to work it out.'

* * *

'Wait till I tell my friends,' Helen grinned. 'They'll never believe what an important job you're doing.'

Mr Roseveare looked at his daughter and shook his head sternly.

'Everyone engaged in the war effort is doing an important job. What I'm doing IS important, but so is what the soldiers are doing, and the factory work the women here in Britain are having to do because their men are at war. Doctors, teachers, farmers, land girls, bus drivers …. everyone who is working for the country is doing important work. So I don't think you should go back to school feeling boastful.'

Helen's father was a strict man, and even though she was now a teenager, a serious talk from him stopped her in her tracks.

Battles Inside and Out

The school in North Wales was a church school, and girls were required to attend services. When she was fourteen years old, Helen felt that she should be confirmed, so she joined a group of girls for confirmation classes.

'Do you understand what confirmation is?' the minister who taught the class asked them.

He didn't wait for an answer.

'When you were children your parents brought you to be baptized. You didn't, of course, know what was happening or have any say in the matter. Your baptism was a sign that you were the children of parents who believed in the Lord Jesus Christ. But you can't go through life relying on your parents' faith. There comes a time when you have to believe for yourself. By asking to be confirmed you are making a statement that you believe in God, and in his Son, Jesus Christ. And in the classes you will attend before confirmation we will study the teachings of the Bible so that you know exactly what it is you are saying you believe.'

Week after week Helen attended his classes and thought through what she heard there.

* * *

'Lights out!' a voice called, and creaks and squeaks of several girls nestling down on their mattresses was heard throughout the dormitory.

But Helen could not sleep.

'The world's a mess,' she thought. 'Millions of people are being killed in the War. Bob's doing war work in this country just now, but maybe he'll be sent abroad one day. The thought scares me. God must be real. He's the only one who can get the world out of the mess it's in. And I need to know all about God. In fact, I need to know God. I'm going to listen to every word the minister says at the confirmation classes.'

* * *

'Helen Roseveare absorbs what I'm saying like a dry sponge,' the minister commented to one of her teachers.

'She also absorbs science, mathematics, drama, sport. In a way she's the ideal pupil.'

'How nice it would be to have a whole class of girls like her,' laughed the minister.

Helen's teacher shook her head. 'I'm not so sure about that. It seems to me that she finds her importance in being good at things, in being first in her form and in winning prizes, rather than accepting that she's important just for her own sake.'

'You mean that she works hard to please people?'

'I think there is a good deal of that in young Helen,' the teacher agreed, 'though when she relaxes she can be quite a mischief and it's not uncommon for her to be sent to the Headmistress for punishment.'

The minister shook his head. 'She sounds a real mixture.'

'And a little mixed up,' added her teacher. 'I hope that we'll be able to help her sort herself out before she leaves us and goes on to do whatever she does after school.'

'She told me she wants to be a missionary,' the man said. 'I must say that was a surprise.'

'It will also surprise the Headmistress! You don't associate missionaries with talking after lights out, running in the corridor or chatting during lessons.'

'I have to admit that these don't seem terrible crimes to me,' the minister smiled. 'But I'm not running a girls' boarding school!'

* * *

Confirmation had a deep effect on Helen in many ways, and one of them was that she began to feel really bad when she told a lie. Lies had come easily to her for years and she had to make a real effort to tell the truth. When she did tell a lie, she now felt an urgent need to own up and apologise.

'This is ridiculous!' one of her teachers said some months later. 'I'm sure that girl would own up to having started the War if she could think of a way in which she might have offended a German when she was at the Berlin Olympics!'

'I know,' smiled her colleague. 'As soon as the Headmistress asks who talked after lights out, her hand is in the air. Everyone breaks school rules,' she said. 'That's what they're there for. But they don't have to ask the Headmistress's personal forgiveness every single time!'

'I heard that she was trying to organise the girls into making formal apologies for all the ways they hurt or upset each other,' the English mistress added. 'It all sounds very holy, but I must say that I don't think it sounds healthy.'

All they said was true. Having told so many lies in the past, it became a matter of great importance to Helen that she told the truth.

'I can only hope to know God if I'm truthful,' she told herself. 'I can only begin to please him if I tell the truth at all times.'

* * *

One thing that was certainly true of the war years was that it was a hard and brutal time. It might have been easy to forget that, safely tucked away in the North Wales countryside as the school was, but so many of the girls had fathers, uncles and brothers fighting in the war that it was always in their thoughts.

When Helen visited her family, who now lived in Kent in the south of England, she had a grandstand view of the Royal Air Force's activities as they flew back and fore across the English Channel.

'They'll be coming soon,' Diana said, 'and if we go out to the tennis court you might get a surprise.'

Wondering what the surprise could be, Helen joined her young sister on the tennis court and waited to see the British aeroplanes flying out on a raid to drop bombs on Germany.

'I wonder what they're aiming for,' thought Helen aloud.

'They're aiming for us!' Jean laughed. 'Try to catch one!'

It took her older sister a minute to realise what was happening. The bombers flew so low overhead each night the men knew the younger Roseveare girls. Not only that, the pilots waved and occasionally threw down sweets from their cockpits! Helen didn't catch one that night, but she became very expert over the weeks she spent at home.

It wasn't long before Helen knew the ritual. The girls waited until they heard the distant roar of an engine and then rushed out to the garden to count the aircraft as they flew overhead, catching sweets if the airmen had any to spare. Then at the first sound of a returning plane they raced outside to count them safely back home again. Of course, the aircraft weren't only British. They saw German planes flying over Kent on their way to drop their lethal bombs on London and heard them returning home too.

'Come on! Come on!' Diana yelled, at the first sound of planes one evening.

'One, two, three, four, five, six ... twenty seven, twenty eight, twenty nine ... the girls counted them as they flew south.

There were no sweets that night, but several pilots gave them a cheery wave as they passed.

'They're very low,' Helen laughed. 'You can almost see the colour of the pilots' eyes!'

'They look so young,' she commented to her mother, when they went back into the house.

'Some of them went straight from school uniforms to RAF uniforms,' she was told. 'In fact, many of them are not much older than Bob.'

Somehow that brought it home to Helen and the thought made her shudder. She could hardly wait to count the planes safely home.

'Twenty six, twenty seven, twenty eight ...'

All three girls held their breath as they watched the southern sky for the plane that was yet to come. They waited forever, at least, that's what it seemed like.

'Who was it?' Diana asked quietly.

Helen struggled with a lump in her throat. Pretending to watch for the plane, she waited until she could speak without crying.

'I think it was the red-head,' she answered, 'the one who threw sweets last night.'

'Are you sure?'

44

'I'm fairly sure. I was watching out for him.'

Nothing more was said and the girls went to their rooms quietly, but inside herself Helen was raging.

'That is so unfair!' she wept into her pillow. 'Why should someone who was smiling and waving a little while ago now be dead?'

Then a terrible thought hit her.

'I know he's dead but his father and mother think he's still alive. Maybe he had a wife or a girlfriend. Maybe he had children.'

But she soon put that thought out of her mind. The pilot who had waved goodbye as he flew to his death was too young to be a father. That was a bad night for Helen Roseveare, for she was learning what it felt like to have a broken heart.

* * *

One day Helen was counting British aircraft when German planes flew up from the south. Her heart raced as she watched them draw closer. Then she stood mesmerised as the pilots fired at each other in the air above her head.

'That one's been hit!' Diana yelled. 'It's coming down!'

'Hurray! It's a German plane,' shouted Helen.

The girls watched as the stricken plane slowly turned in the air, smoke billowing from a broken wing, then plummeted to the ground. Mrs Roseveare, who was involved with the Red Cross, was on duty that night. When she came home, quite exhausted, the girls told her what they had seen.

'I know,' she said wearily. 'And the poor young man didn't survive, though we did all we could to save him.'

Helen's eyes flashed.

'Why?' she demanded. 'He was an enemy! He was fighting British pilots and trying to kill them. And his plane was loaded with bombs to kill people just like us!'

'Calm down!' said her mother sharply. 'And think what you're saying.'

Helen's sat quietly, though her breathing showed what a fury she was in.

'Now listen to me,' Mrs Roseveare insisted. 'We're at war with Germany, not with individual German soldiers, sailors or airmen. That young man whose life I tried to save tonight wasn't fighting by choice, any more than most British airmen. All he was doing was obeying orders.'

'But ...' Helen tried to interrupt.

'There are no buts,' her mother said firmly. 'It's a pity you didn't see that young man before he died. Maybe then you would have realised that he was someone's son, someone's brother, perhaps someone's husband and father. He has a whole family back home in Germany who are hoping and praying that he'll come home safe again. And he never will. Remember that next time you shout *hurray* when a

German plane's shot down. Now, I think you should go to your room and think about that.'

'I'm sorry,' said Helen quietly. 'I'm truly sorry.'

In the hours that followed Helen lay in bed alone with her thoughts. And the thought that went round and round in her mind was this: there was no difference between the young German who had been killed a few miles away and the red-headed pilot who had waved to her from the plane, never to come back. All that made them enemies was where they had been born. Helen did some growing up that night.

* * *

'London is beautiful and awful,' Helen thought, as she made one of her many wartime journeys between home and school. 'There's the River Thames winding through it like a silver ribbon and there are the slums, where children scurry about like mice. Some places seem to be no better than when Charles Dickens wrote *Oliver Twist* a hundred years ago.'

The bus on which she was travelling turned a corner and Helen found herself looking out on a bombsite.

'There was a three storey building here last time I passed,' she thought. 'It must have been bombed just after that because wild flowers are already growing in the rubble.'

From under an old abandoned door a little boy peered out, unaware of an older lad behind him.

'Gottcha!' she heard the taller boy say, as he rushed back to his den. 'You're it!'

Helen grinned.

'It may be the ruin of their home for all I know,' she thought, 'but these boys certainly know how to make the most of it for a game of hide and seek.'

Suddenly the bus filled with sound as the local air raid warning ripped through the air. For a split second nobody moved. Then some women sprang to their feet, ran along the corridor of the bus and jumped off while it was still moving.

'Where are they going?' Helen asked herself. 'Where will I go?'

The women raced for the building nearest the bus. Thrusting the door open, they crowded in and slammed it shut behind them.

Horrified, Helen heard a bomb whining down through the air.

'Where is it? Where's it going to land?'

Her eyes widened when the terrible truth hit her - the bomb was heading straight for the building in which the women were sheltering. The crash was something terrible, and there are no words to describe the pain Helen felt as she thought of the women inside. As the building burst into a blazing inferno she could hear the women screaming. Almost immediately the men from the Civil Defence were on the scene doing everything they could to help.

Helen was not the only teenager in Britain - or

in Germany, for that matter - to ask herself huge questions, questions too big to be answered. But she asked them all the same. 'Why are these things happening? Why are people being injured and killed? Why do wars and famines and earthquakes happen? Her mind and her heart were full of whys. 'Surely God can do something to help,' she thought desperately. 'If God exists, surely he'll help.'

* * *

'Where are you off to?' Helen was asked, as she took her bicycle from the bicycle shed at school.

'I'm going to a Christian camp,' she answered.

It was the summer of 1941, the Second World War was still raging, and Helen needed to find answers to the questions that troubled her. Although there was a serious side to camp it was also great fun. It suited the sporty Helen very well indeed.

'You're good at games!' someone laughed, when she won yet again.

How wonderful the happy laughter sounded.

'Are you coming for a walk this afternoon?' It was almost as though everything was right with the world.

'Look at the wild flowers. They're beautiful!'

So they were. There was still beauty in the world despite all the ugly things that war brought with it. But it wasn't the games or the walks or the beautiful countryside that meant most to Helen.

'Time for chapel,' a girl said. 'Are you coming?'

Nothing could keep Helen away from chapel, and from Father Charles Preston, the Anglican monk who took the short meetings there.

'Father Preston almost shines when he talks about Jesus,' she commented to a friend.

'I know,' was the reply. 'I think that's because he loves the Lord Jesus Christ so much.'

The more Helen learned from Father Preston, the more she wanted to know. And the more she wanted to know, the more God taught her. It was as though she was hungrier to learn about God than she was for her dinner every day. And that was saying something! Before camp ended Helen went to speak to a leader about how she felt. She asked God to forgive her sins and felt she was floating on air. Finding a place to sit in the dimly lit chapel, she opened a hymn book and read the words of a hymn.

> *'Take my life, and let it be*
> *Consecrated, Lord, to Thee ...*
> *Take myself, and I will be*
> *Ever, only, all for Thee.'*

And when she left the building, Helen felt she could have jumped over the rooftops!

* * *

'Are you off home now?' she was asked when camp was over.

'Yes, I am.'

'What are you going to do in the holidays?'

'I'm not sure,' Helen replied. 'But I must go round all my family and say sorry for all the wrong things I've done to them over the years.'

Helen did that, much to the surprise of her sisters! And each time she did something wrong from then on she aimed to apologise as soon as she realised what she had done.

In the three years that followed, until Helen Roseveare left school, she tried hard to be a Christian. *But,* deep in her heart there was still an empty space and nothing she did could fill it. She helped in a Christian centre, spent time with Christian people, and tried to be good, tried to be kind, tried to be forgiving, tried and tried and tried and tried. Helen tried until she was completely exhausted, and there was still an empty place in her heart.

* * *

'So you've been accepted to study medicine at Cambridge,' a teacher said, just before Helen left school in the summer of 1944. 'Congratulations!'

'Well done, Helen!' friends said at the school prize-giving. 'You've come out top as usual!'

'You're a real credit to us,' Mr Roseveare told his daughter. 'I'm proud of you.'

'And so am I,' her mother added. 'You've done so well, dear!'

Compliments and congratulations came from

every side, and a warm glow comforted Helen, but it was sad to say goodbye to school friends.

'We'll write to each other,' they all promised. 'Don't let's lose touch.'

A strange mixture of excitement and fear filled most of their hearts at the thought of leaving their safe and comfortable girls' boarding school and going out into the big wide world.

* * *

'Let's meet in London for a meal and a visit to the theatre before you go off to Cambridge,' suggested Mr Roseveare.

Helen grinned. 'That would be lovely?' she said. 'Where would we go?'

'There's a musical on this summer. Would you like that?'

So on a hot summer day, Helen met her father in the centre of London and had a grown-up time with him. As they sat side by side in the theatre watching the musical show - which was very funny indeed - Helen laughed as she'd not laughed for a very long time. In the darkness of the theatre it was easy to forget the seriously scary thought of studying medicine at Cambridge, and the even scarier thought that there was a war still going on all around them.

Medical student

It was the end of July 1944, and eighteen-year-old Helen felt as nervous as a kitten when she opened the door of room 8a in Clough Hall, Cambridge University.

'Help! I don't know a single person here!'

Looking round the room, she noticed that it was quite small. Her trunk was pushed against the door that joined her room to the one next door to keep it shut.

'Why am I here?' she asked herself. 'I'll never fit in!'

Closing the door firmly behind her, Helen decided she had to do something – so she took the straps off her trunk and began to unpack.

'I'll put everything on the bed to start with then decide where to put things.'

She unpacked her clothes and books and toilet things, laying them all side by side on the bed, and put her shoes on the floor beside it.

'I'll put the books here,' she decided, spying two small shelves on the wall above the bed. 'And I suppose this chest of drawers is for my clothes.'

As she packed her old school shirts into one drawer and her underwear into another, she wished

- just for a minute – that she didn't have to wear her school clothes until they wore out.

'But it can't be helped,' she decided. 'I can't expect my parents to give me a whole new set of clothes just because I've come to university.'

* * *

'I look an absolute fright!' Helen moaned, when she caught sight of herself in the mirror as she passed with an armful of clothes.

The hair in her pigtails was making a bid for freedom and her face was as pale as could be.

'What's that?' she said, noticing a card tucked into the side of her mirror. Taking it out, she read it aloud.

'If you don't know anyone, and have nowhere to go after supper, come and have coffee in my room, no. 12, at 8 pm. Dorothy.'

When she tried to read the card again, Helen couldn't. Her eyes had filled up with tears of relief at someone wanting to know her, and of fear and excitement and homesickness all at the same time.

A bell rang. Panic!

'What do I do now?' Helen thought.

She opened her room door to discover a line of girls all going in the same direction. Closing her door behind her, she joined the line.

'They all know each other,' she thought, 'and I don't know anyone. Help!'

Eventually they arrived in the dining hall and Helen copied what everyone else was doing.

'You're new,' someone said.

'Yes,' Helen agreed and then was lost for words.

'Not a bad meal considering rationing,' a girl commented kindly.

Helen swallowed what was in her mouth.

'It's very nice,' she agreed, but couldn't think of anything else to say.

There was noise all around her. Girls chatted to each other across the table ... but Helen chatted to nobody. It was almost as though she wasn't really there – and she wished she wasn't. After dinner she was so unhappy that she decided to write to her mother and say she was coming home!

* * *

At five minutes to eight Helen washed her face, tidied her hair and set out for room 12.

Knock. Knock.

'Come in!'

There was smoke everywhere! Through the haze Helen could see a student kneeling on the floor trying to light the fire.

'Can you make a fire?' a voice asked through the smoke?

'I think so,' said Helen, joining Dorothy on the floor.

Between them they had the fire going in no time, and as they sat on either side of it drinking smoky coffee, Helen's fears began to fade a little.

'I'll call for you in the morning and we can have breakfast together, if you like,' suggested Dorothy as they parted.

'I'd like that,' Helen said.

She had made a friend.

When Saturday came she met some other girls, and even went out with them punting on the River Cam.

'I'm glad I didn't write and say I was coming straight back home,' Helen smiled, as she went to bed that night.

Over the weeks that followed, Helen realised that she had developed two groups of friends, one that centred on sport and the other - including Dorothy - who were Christians.

'Where do you scurry off to before hall?' she asked Dorothy one day.

Her friend smiled.

'Some of us meet to pray for a short time,' she explained, 'and one night a week we have a Bible study together. Would you like to join us?'

'Yes, please,' Helen grinned. She liked Dorothy very much indeed.

That night fairly took the young medical student by surprise.

'How come you all know the Bible so well?' she asked her friend in amazement as they drank some cocoa together. 'You don't just know what the Bible says, you know where to find things in it!'

Dorothy grinned. 'You should come along to the Bible study every week and get to know it too.'

* * *

'Do you want to join us at the Christian Union?' Dorothy asked, some days later.

Helen agreed, and the pair of them cycled to the meeting and left their bikes outside.

'Well, that was an interesting evening,' thought Helen, as she prepared to go to bed that night. 'Imagine someone stealing my bicycle when I was at Christian Union! It doesn't seem fair somehow.'

* * *

By the time Helen's second term at Cambridge was coming to an end she was attending Christian Union meetings, the Bible study group and prayer meetings, as well as any missionary meetings that were held.

'Come in,' Helen called when someone knocked at her door.

A fellow student opened the door and entered. 'What are you reading?' she asked.

'It's the Bible,' Helen explained. 'Have you ever read it?'

Her visitor shook her head.

'I haven't read the Bible since I went to Sunday school,' she added.

'Phew,' said Helen. 'When I started reading it a few weeks ago it was a real slog. I thought I'd never get through it. But now,' her eyes shone, 'I can't get enough of it. The Bible makes so much sense.'

'Everyone to their own thing,' commented the other girl. 'I'll go and leave you in peace to get on with your reading.'

* * *

'You look like a cat whose cream has been stolen,' someone said on seeing Helen one day in December. 'Aren't you looking forward to Christmas?'

'I was. But I've just heard that my young sister has mumps and I'd best not go home for the holiday.'

'Oh, that is a shame. You'll have to find somewhere interesting to go.'

'But where?' wondered Helen, as she walked along the corridor. 'I can't just invite myself to someone's home at Christmas time.'

Before she had time to be upset about it, two Christian friends each invited her to their homes for a week. That took care of the first two weeks of the holiday, but there was still another ten days to fill.

* * *

'We think you should come to the houseparty at Mount Hermon Bible College,' said Dorothy. 'You'll know plenty of people there and you'll enjoy it such a lot.'

'I don't know,' Helen replied, thinking how little money she had left from her allowance.

'Look,' insisted Dorothy. 'Here are the train times and this is the timetable for the houseparty. See you there.'

Helen did go, and much to her surprise she discovered it was a gathering of young women who were there to train as camp leaders for Christian camps to be held that Easter and summer!

'It's absolutely freezing,' the students agreed, wrapping themselves in their blankets for a Bible study.

The temperature was freezing, quite literally, but the fun and the friendships were warm and Helen loved it. But all the time she knew that she was different. The others all seemed to know the Lord Jesus while she just knew about him. In truth, they seemed to be living in a different world from her, and she longed to be part of it.

* * *

'Would you like salt?' Helen was asked, as they ate their last dinner together before leaving the Bible College.

'No thanks,' was the reply, for her mind was on the discussion that was going on around her.

The discussion turned to an argument which became bad-tempered, with Helen among those who lost control. Suddenly, realising what had happened, she jumped to her feet, left the room and ran upstairs to her dorm. Throwing herself on her bed, she wept like a child.

'I'm hopeless,' she cried. 'I'm just a failure.' Helen had never in her life felt so sad and so lonely.

'God,' she wept, 'if you exist please make yourself real to me.'

Raising her eyes, she looked through her tears to a Bible text hanging on the wall opposite her.

'*Be still, and know that I am God*' (Psalm 46:10) she read quietly.

Then the Lord spoke right into her heart. It was as though she was being told to stop rushing around looking for him, to stop trying to understand him, just to be still and know that the Lord is God. The peace and joy that flooded Helen's mind and heart was something she'd never known before. Now she knew, SHE KNEW, that she was a Christian. At last, after years of searching and struggling, Helen Roseveare had found what she was looking for. Jesus was her Saviour! So much of what she had read in the Bible suddenly fell into place. She was a new person - and she couldn't stop smiling! Downstairs Helen went to join the others.

'Look at her!' several of her friends thought, as they turned in her direction. 'Her face is shining!'

'Let's sing!' the leader suggested, and chorus after chorus rang out.

Helen knew none of them, but she was far too happy to let that bother her.

'Does anyone want to tell us what God has done for her this week?' asked the person leading the meeting.

There was an uncomfortably long silence. In the midst of the silence Helen knew she had to tell her friends what had happened to her. She opened her mouth to speak and could think of nothing to say. How do you put a miracle into words?

'I ... I ....' long pause, 'I just want to say that I've met with God and that my sins have been forgiven.'

What joy filled the room!

'Helen,' said Dr Graham Scroggie, the houseparty's Bible teacher. 'Knowing Jesus is just the beginning, and there's a long journey ahead. My prayer for you is that you will go on through the years to know his power. It is perhaps in God's plan for you to suffer for your Saviour as he suffered for you.' He then took her Bible, and wrote a verse in it that says just that.

'*That I may know him and the power of his resurrection, and the fellowship of his sufferings, being made conformable unto his death*' (Philippians 3:10 AV)

The following day everyone left for home and Helen was able to go home too as all danger of her catching mumps had passed.

'I'm going to buy myself a Scripture Union badge

before I go,' she decided, 'as a sign to anyone who sees me that I'm a Christian.'

A short time later, on the train home, she sat opposite a man who noticed the badge right away! 'What does your badge stand for?' he asked.

Helen jumped. 'It means that I'm a member of Scripture Union.'

'And what does that involve?'

'Members read the Bible every day because they believe that God will use that to help them live as he wants them to live' Helen explained, feeling just a little awkward about this very public conversation, for the train carriage was full.

'Why do you believe that?'

'Because ….' and Helen had to raise her voice over the noise of the train, 'the Bible is the Word of God.'

Question after question followed and Helen tried to answer them all. The other people in the carriage did not seem to be best pleased at having their comfortable train journey interrupted by the conversation she and the man were having. Helen blushed in embarrassment, but she did her best and even described how she had become a Christian just the night before.

A whistle sounded and the train rumbled to a halt.

'Thank goodness for that!' Helen thought, grabbing her bags.

But as she walked along the platform someone laid a hand on her shoulder.

'Oh,' she said, 'it's you.'

The man whose questions she had struggled to answer smiled kindly.

'When I saw that your badge and Bible were spanking new, I wanted to give you the opportunity to talk about your faith in front of all the people in the railway carriage. Never be embarrassed about your faith in Jesus,' he said. 'Go on telling others about him as you told me today. That's what we Christians should all be doing.'

* * *

'What are you going to do when you finish university?' Helen was asked quite regularly.

Others thought they knew.

'You'll work in a hospital, I imagine. Being a family doctor is perhaps not really a suitable job for a young woman.'

'Of course you'll just work for a year or two and then marry and settle down to have a family.'

And to all of this the young medical student answered, 'I'm going to be a missionary.'

From the age of eight Helen had said the same. Mind you, it was only since coming to Cambridge that she really knew what being a missionary was all about!

* * *

'How can I know what God wants me to do?' Helen asked Mildred Mitchell, one of the older girls in the Christian Union. Mildred introduced Helen to her father, Fred Mitchell, who was responsible for caring for a great many missionaries in China. Helen repeated her question to him.

Fred held up his hand.

'Read your Bible every day,' he said, pointing to his finger. 'God speaks through his Word. Secondly, pray every day. Talk all your problems over with the Lord.' He pointed to his next finger as he spoke. 'Thirdly,' he went on, 'ask advice from older Christians. Fourthly,' Mr Mitchell pointed to his fourth finger, 'take your circumstances into account, things like your health, money and family. When God speaks to you, he will give you peace.'

From then on that was how Helen found what the Lord wanted her to do. However, she still had a lot to learn about prayer. For example, although Mildred's father had told her to talk all her problems over with the Lord, there were some problems that she didn't think were quite proper to pray about. One of these came to light during the summer of 1945, when she was Medical Officer at a camp for girls.

* * *

'Let's play a game of rounders, girls!' the camp leader shouted.

There were screams of delight. The previous game had been only just won by the blue team, and the red team was determined to win this time round.

'Wow!' yelled the blue team when the first in to bat for the reds missed the ball.

But she didn't miss the second one.

'Hurray!' the reds screamed. 'Run for it!'

The batter ran to the first stump, on to the second and then looked to see where the fielders were. They were well away!

'Run! Run!' her friends shouted. 'Go for it!'

She ran on to the third stump, touched it with the bat and then made a dash for home. The fielder who had caught the ball threw it to a team mate who was right beside home. She caught the ball and dumped it on home, but the batter was there before her.

'Hip! Hip hurray!' yelled the reds delightedly.

And so the game went on … interrupted by one girl after another having to leave the field to go to the toilet! As she was the camp's Medical Officer, Helen enquired and discovered that many of the fifty campers had upset tummies.

'We're going to need more toilet rolls,' she told the camp leaders. 'We've nearly run out!'

Before anything could be done about that a message came from the local minister with the most wonderful news.

'Japan has been defeated. The Second World War is over! The world is at peace!'

What joy!

'We're having a service in the village to thank God for the victory. Would you all like to come along?'

Of course they would!

Helen's thrill at the news about the end of the war suddenly turned to panic. The shop would be closed when the service was over and she'd not be able to buy toilet rolls!

'What will we do about it?' she asked the camp leader, during a short meeting that followed.

And Helen was quite shocked when she heard the leader reminding the Lord that they needed toilet paper urgently. It had never crossed her mind that God would care about such things as that!

* * *

The campers went with their leaders to church and joined in the service of thanksgiving. What happiness there was that day!

'My dad will soon be home,' one girl laughed as they walked back to camp. 'I can hardly believe it!'

'And my brothers will come back,' another added. 'I've missed them so much.'

'Excuse me,' a man said, stopping Helen on the road. 'I just want to say how pleased we are to have a Christian camp in our village. It was especially good to have you with us at the service.'

'Thank you very much,' Helen replied. 'That's kind of you.'

'I'm the local grocer,' the man added. 'If there's anything I can do to help you, please let me know.' Helen's eyes lit up.

'There is,' she said, smiling broadly. 'We have a little problem of a tummy bug and a serious lack of toilet paper.'

The man smiled kindly. 'Don't worry about it. I'll see to that.'

Half an hour later twelve toilet rolls arrived at the camp.

'What an answer to prayer,' Helen thought. 'I would never have thought of praying for toilet rolls. How good God is!'

* * *

Helen's work with young people didn't only take her to camp. When she moved from Cambridge to London to continue training to be a doctor, she became a Girl Crusaders' Union (GCU) leader.

'May we use a room behind the garage for meetings?' Helen asked her mother, as the family home was now in London and she was based there for the time being.

'I don't see why not,' Mrs Roseveare replied, 'except that it's in no fit state to be used for anything.'

'That's all right,' said Helen. 'Some Crusaders will help me clean it up.'

And two boys arrived the following week to do just that.

* * *

'Right, boys,' Helen laughed, 'where do we begin?'

'We could start by taking all the rubbish outside,' one suggested.

'Or by brushing down the ceiling to get rid of those miles of cobwebs.'

'It's just an earth floor,' pointed out Helen. 'We'll have to do something about that.'

'You mean cement it?' a boy asked.

Helen nodded.

'This is serious cleaning,' joked the lad. 'But at least we'll see a difference when it's done.'

They worked incredibly hard, and by the end of their efforts the ceiling and walls had been brushed down and a cement floor laid.

'Do you know what I'd like to do?' one lad teased, when the last bit of cement was levelled. 'I'd like to put my foot in it and leave a mark for history.'

His friend laughed. 'Just you think again!'

Later on two or three thirteen-year-old girls took over from the boys.

'What do you want us to do?' they asked, looking around.

Helen smiled. 'Are you any good with paint brushes?'

Soon they were all busily painting the doors and window frames.

'What now?' she was asked when the paintwork was done.

'We need something to sit on, and somewhere to put our books and Bibles.'

'You mean tables and chairs?' queried one of the girls.

Helen laughed. 'Sort of,' she admitted, pointing to logs and planks of wood.

'We've to make them ourselves!' the youngsters laughed.

'More balance them than make them,' Helen pointed out.

'Done!' the girls announced, when benches and a table-of-sorts were eventually put together. 'We're finished!'

'Not quite. I think we need something on the wall on which we can mark competition scores - a kind of thermometer.'

That was done.

* * *

'Would you like to come and see our meeting room?' Helen asked her mother when the girls had all left for home at the end of their week of very hard work.

Mrs Roseveare raised her eyebrows. 'I'll be interested to see what you've made of it.'

The two women walked out of the house and round behind the garage.

'I feel like a little girl taking my mummy to see my sandcastle,' thought Helen, greatly amused at the very idea.

'Well, well,' laughed her mother. 'Who would have believed it?'

Her daughter grinned. 'It's ideal for a GCU meeting. Isn't it?'

'Yes, my dear. I have to admit that along with your young friends, you've worked wonders.'

Helen's only free day was Saturday. So beside the Sunday afternoon group when four girls and their leaders met together, Helen also met with eight to ten girls on Saturday afternoons for 'extra' Bible study.

Called to the Congo

'You'll make a good doctor,' a patient told Helen, near the end of her training. 'Do you hope to find a job in a hospital here in London?'

'No,' she replied. 'I'm hoping to go abroad as a missionary doctor.'

Her patient's eyes opened wide. 'Have you been accepted for missionary training?'

Helen said she had begun that process. 'I move to WEC Headquarters next month and will be there for six months. By then they'll know whether I'm suitable or not.'

'What is WEC?'

'The letters stand for Worldwide Evangelisation Crusade, but it's always just known as WEC.'

'I wish you well,' the patient smiled.

* * *

Monday 15th January 1951 was Helen's first day in WEC Headquarters as a missionary candidate.

'Your room is on the first floor,' she was told. 'You're sharing with a Swedish girl. I'm sure you'll get on well.'

'Of course we will,' thought Helen. 'I've got to show that I can get on with anyone.'

The first day passed in a flurry of excitement. It was so different from that terrible first day in Cambridge when all Helen wanted to do was pack up and go home.

* * *

'You all have chores to do,' the candidates were told next morning. 'Remember that they are part of your training. When you go to the mission field you'll have to do whatever job you're given, nice or nasty.'

The students wondered what was coming!

'Helen,' said Elizabeth, who was in charge of the candidates, 'I'd like you to wash out the cement floors in the girls' toilets.'

Armed with a bucket, brush and everything she would need, young Dr Roseveare headed for the toilets. She smiled as she walked, for it was probably the first time in her life that she'd ever had to do housework! Getting down on her knees Helen scrubbed one toilet until it was as clean as could be.

'There!' she said, sitting back on her heels to admire her work. 'Now for the other one.'

As she scrubbed the second floor, someone went into the first toilet with muddy feet and ruined all her work! When the second toilet was as clean as could be, Helen looked in the first one again and her heart sank. It didn't look as if it had been cleaned at all!

'I'll have to do it again,' she thought.

Determined to make a good impression on Elizabeth, Helen once again went down on her knees to scrub toilet number one… and as she did it someone came in with mud on her shoes and used the other one! For just a minute it seemed funny, then it didn't seem funny at all. For what felt like ages Helen went from toilet to toilet scrubbing the floors after each person left. She felt as though she was being chased by the devil of dirty feet.

'What are you doing?' asked Elizabeth, who had come to see how she was getting on.

'I'll never get them clean,' Helen said, with tears in her voice if not in her eyes. 'Every time I finish one, someone comes in and messes it up and I have to do it all over again.'

'For whom are you scrubbing the floor?' asked Elizabeth quietly.

That nearly made Helen cry.

'I'm scrubbing it for *you*. You told me to do it.'

Elizabeth looked deep into the young woman's eyes. 'No, my dear,' she said. 'If you are doing it for me, you may as well go home. You'll never satisfy me. But you're doing it for the Lord, and he saw the first time you cleaned it. The dirt that's there now is tomorrow's dirt, not today's.'

Helen felt a great weight fall from her shoulders. She had begun to learn one of the biggest lessons that missionary training can teach – things should be done for Jesus, not to please other people.

* * *

Missionary training was not easy. It covered many different subjects in several different places, including a year in Belgium studying French and tropical medicine. But the day dawned when Dr Helen Roseveare, having been accepted by WEC to work in the Congo, said goodbye to her family and friends and climbed aboard the *Dunnottar Castle* in London Docks. Her voyage included diverting to pick up a sailor who needed his appendix removed, and rescuing nine men who were drifting to almost certain death!

* * *

'My feet are standing on African soil!' Helen thrilled at the thought, when she eventually walked down the gang plank on to the port of Mombasa in Kenya some weeks later. 'I can hardly take it in!'

The sights, the smells, the heat, the noise ... all were new, strange and very, very exciting! It was by another boat, this time a small steamer, that Helen eventually arrived in the Congo to be welcomed by Jack Scholes, her mission field leader, along with one other white man and two Congolese gentlemen.

'You'll find the next part of the journey interesting,' Jack told her.

And it was. The road twisted and turned round hairpin bends all the way to Nyankunde, where they were to stay for a day or two before travelling to their final destination.

* * *

'Doctor! Doctor!'

The call came in the middle of the night, and the Nyankunde doctor was away.

'Will you go?' Helen was asked.

Quick as could be she dressed and was taken through the forest to a remote village.

'What's that noise?' she asked, when wailing could be heard through the trees.

'I'm afraid we're too late,' was the answer. 'That's death-wailing.'

'Follow me,' the young doctor was told.

And she followed her companion into the darkness of a mud hut crowded with people. When she reached her first patient in the Congo, the man was already dead.

'Who were all the women?' she asked, as they made their way back to Nyankunde.

'They were the man's wives and other family members gathered to mourn his death.'

'I'm sorry we didn't get there soon enough,' said Helen.

Her companion shook his head. 'We got there as soon as we could.'

From Nyankunde Helen and the others made their way in a lorry and a pick-up truck to Ibambi.

'What an amazing country,' thought the new young missionary, turning her head this way and that to see all there was to see. 'We've come through forests and village clearings. We've driven through rivers and over vast grasslands.'

'Nearly there!' Jack Scholes said. 'And I imagine there'll be a fine welcome awaiting you.'

Helen could hardly believe her eyes!

'Look at that!' she cried. 'The trees have all been decorated, and there's a huge red "Welcome to Ibambi" banner with the words written in cotton wool.'

'They must have used all of the hospital's supply of cotton wool!' laughed Jack.

Singing and dancing, clapping and laughing surrounded the newcomer. But all the noise faded when Pastor Ndugu stepped forward.

'The Church of Jesus Christ in Congo, and we her elders, welcome you, our child, into our midst,' he said solemnly.

'Our child!' The words went straight to Helen's heart. 'They're welcoming me as their child!' she thought, hardly able to take in the wonder of it. 'I belong to these dear people. I've come home!'

* * *

'My day begins at 5.10 am,' Helen wrote to a friend, 'as I've to be at the Bible school for morning prayers by 6.30 am. After that there's breakfast and family prayers, and by then it's 9 am and time to open the dispensary. That sounds very grand but it's actually just a bare room with a cement floor and a tin roof.

The shelves are just boards balanced on tea-chests. In fact, if you remember our little GCU room behind the garage at my mother's home you've almost got the picture.'

Laying down her pen, Helen wondered what to say next.

'Patients arrive in their dozens, and they have such a variety of problems. As we can't speak to each other because I don't have Swahili and they don't speak French or English, they have to point to whatever is wrong and then I poke and prod to make some kind of diagnosis. Of course, sometimes it's quite obvious. You've no idea the number of running sores I've seen since I came here. I don't have a helper yet, but I hope to have one soon.'

* * *

Jack and Jessie Scholes shared their home with Helen, and they shared her vision too.

'It is wonderful to see the medical work starting,' Jessie said, as they drank a cup of tea together one evening. 'What you're doing is just a small beginning, but I believe God will build it up to be a great medical work.'

Helen couldn't envisage a great medical work. To her it was a great enough miracle that she got through each day when so many patients were queueing to see her. By Easter time the Lord had provided Helen with a helper, Elizabeth Naganimi. The only problem was

that Helen spoke English, French and a little Swahili
and her new helper spoke the Bangala language!

* * *

Over the months that followed Helen settled down
at Ibambi.

When a missionary conference was held in
January 1954, she was able to tell those who gathered
what her vision was for the work.

'We need to train national workers to do
the medical work. There can only ever be a few
missionaries in an area, and we come and go. If we
train national workers they will remain and then the
work will build up and continue.'

'Are you saying that we should open a nursing
school?' she was asked.

Helen nodded. 'Yes, that's exactly what I'm
suggesting.'

'And where do you suggest it should be based?'

Puzzled that the question was even asked, Helen
replied, 'Ibambi, of course.'

The discussion went this way and that until Helen
felt quite overwhelmed.

'We think that a nursing school would be better
based in Nebobongo, where the leprosy work is
done,' she was told eventually. 'That's only seven
miles away.'

Helen's head spun. Seven miles! But seven miles
of the most difficult travelling possible!

God spoke to Helen's heart and told her to be calm and to wait. In the meantime a tiny nurses' training school was started with just eight young men. None were well educated. In fact, John Mangadima, who was the most qualified of them all, had only done seven years of primary schooling.

'Goodness me!' a visitor said, just nine months later. 'The medical work here is growing like a beanstalk! What's been happening?'

Helen took great delight in walking her visitor through the new facilities.

'Here are our two wards,' she said, indicating a whitewashed mud building. 'The twenty-four bed ward is for women and children and we have a small eight-bed ward for men.'

'And your other facilities?'

'Oh yes,' beamed Helen. 'We have an area for seeing patients, somewhere for drugs and a maternity room as well as a dispensary.'

'How has this all come together so soon?'

Helen laughed. 'The local church people did most of it, along with the boys learning to be nurses and the patients themselves.'

'The patients! Well I am surprised!' exclaimed her visitor.

* * *

'Do you think we have any chance of passing our exams?' John Mangadima asked, just one year later.

'Of course you do,' Helen told the seven who were about to get into her van to drive to Pawa where they would sit the dreaded examinations.

At Pawa they were in for a shock.

'All the other students speak French!' John told Helen. 'If they ask us the questions in French we'll not understand what they are saying.'

Helen prayed hard. And when their turn came, the Ibambi boys were questioned in Swahili. It seemed a long time until the results were read out that afternoon. One of Helen's students had come first, another was third and four others passed! Only one did not, and he was asked to sit it again the following year. The car fairly rocked as they wove their way home, with its driver and all seven passengers singing and laughing and praising God inside it.

'We have our first very own national assistant nurses!' Helen told her friends when they reached Ibambi.

She didn't really need to spread the news. Their happy faces had done that already!

* * *

'I would like to talk to you, Helen,' Jack Scholes said the following day. 'There's something I have to tell you.'

Helen looked up. This sounded serious.

'The Mission Field Committee has decided that the time has come to move the medical work to

Nebobongo. They would like you to start the move later this week.'

Young Dr Roseveare was stunned into silence … but only for a minute … then she had plenty to say, not much of it very helpful. It took her a little time to realise that it was the Lord who was moving the work to Nebobongo, and she had to go where he was sending her. On 30th October 1955 the move was made.

* * *

As they drove the long seven miles from Ibambi to Nebobongo, Helen thought of the history of the place. War had left its scars.

'There was once a good medical work going there, caring for hundreds of leprosy patients,' she remembered, 'with dispensary buildings and neat rows of mud huts for the patients, along with gardens where mealies and vegetables would have been grown to feed them. Now what's there?' Her heart sank at the present devastation and neglect … then rose again. 'Well, Florence Stebbing still runs a maternity unit and there's the orphanage work too. It's a pity so much of it has been left to grow derelict.' Helen straightened her back and thought of the amazing things she had seen God do in the past. 'Yes, much of it is derelict now,' she said to herself, 'but not for long. Let's see what the Lord can do.'

* * *

Helen was no sooner in Nebobongo than she was down to work. 'Let's work out the possibilities,' she said to three of her Congolese colleagues.

With measuring tapes, paper and pencils they set out to walk over the land.

'What are the most important things?' one of the men asked.

'Well,' said Helen, 'if we are going to start by using the orphanage as a hospital while we build other wards, we'll have to try to find homes for the children.'

'Many of them have family members who could take them into their homes,' suggested her friend. 'That would release the building for hospital use.'

One of the other men had an idea. 'If we move the workmen's village to a healthier part of the compound they won't suffer so much sickness.'

Helen smiled. 'That's a really good idea. There's a good flat space right at the western end of the land.'

Pleased that his suggestion had been taken up, he had a further thought.

'If we want to keep our workmen, we'll need to provide a school for their children.'

All heads nodded in agreement and they walked again over the land looking for a suitable site for a school.

As Helen discussed plans with the men she thought just how different things were back home in England. But was England home? No, not really. By then she felt more at home in the Congo. She felt as though she'd been adopted by the Congolese Christians and was part of their family.

'In England we'd discuss our ideas then call in an architect to make up plans. We'd then employ a project manager to do all the work, from buying bricks, cement and roof tiles to window panes, nails and door handles.' She smiled at the thought. 'Here we'll draw up our own plans, make our own bricks, cut down trees for the wood we need and put up the buildings with our very own hands.'

God did do wonderful things there and over time a hospital complex was built – all mud buildings with tin roofs. Elephant grass gave way to hospital buildings. Scrub was cleared for a school. Trees were felled to make space for workers' and nurses' homes. Patients were treated, children taught and those orphans who stayed on at Nebobongo cared for. Nurses were trained and babies born – about forty of them each month! It was busy, busy, busy! From time to time it was so busy that it got on top of Helen.

* * *

'Eye clinic today,' she thought, as she woke up one Thursday morning.

By nine o'clock she was ready. The room in which she would see her patients was darkened, her instruments were laid out ready and the first patient came. It wasn't too busy a morning and Helen was able to get her instruments packed away in time to do her late-morning ward round.

'An old lady has been brought here so that you can look at her eyes,' Helen was told, as she was seeing her hospital patients.

Tired, overworked and stressed, Helen looked up at her houseboy who had come with the message.

'Where does the lady come from?' she asked.

'From a nearby village,' was the reply.

'Tell her to come back next week at 9 am when the clinic starts and I'll see her then.'

The houseboy left the ward and sent the old lady away.

* * *

'May I speak to you,' John Mangadima said, a short time later.

'Of course,' Helen answered. 'What is it?'
John looked unusually serious.

'Could you not see that that old lady was blind?' he asked. 'She waited all morning at the roadside in her village for someone to lead her to Nebobongo to see the Christian doctor who heals people.'

Helen felt sick at the thought of what she had done.

'She is a soul for whom Christ died,' John went on, 'and you turned her away harshly. Would Christ have done that?'

Buildings were important, Helen knew that, but

people were much more important than mud bricks and tin roofs. From time to time John had to remind her of that.

* * *

While there were very hard times at Nebobongo, and many days when Helen was utterly exhausted as she tried to do far too many things at once, there were also wonderful times when God especially blessed the people there. God met with some of her African friends in a very wonderful way and they prayed that Helen would be given the same blessings. After a very long time she was. Thrilled with the special feeling of God being so close, Helen cycled to the hospital where three of her student nurses met her. Smiling from ear to ear, they praised God that Helen was filled with the joy of the Lord.

'How did you know what had happened to me?' she asked.

The young men looked at each other and smiled.

'We've been praying for you every day for four years, asking the Lord to fill you with the same joy that he had given us. Now he has answered our prayers.'

That night, as Helen settled down in bed, she thought of her Congolese friends. She had come as their missionary, yet it was they who had prayed that she should be filled with the joy God had given to them. She fell asleep with a warm glow inside her, the warm glow that comes from being truly loved.

Rebellion!

It was 20th May 1960. Helen, who had spent some time back in Britain, was once again boarding a ship that would take her from London to Mombasa, from where she would travel on to Nebobongo.

'Have you had a good rest?' a fellow passenger asked, when she heard that Helen was a missionary home on leave. 'I know you work hard when you're overseas, but you do get long holidays when you come home.'

Helen smiled. 'I'm not sure that you could call my time in Britain holiday,' she said. 'Much of it has been spent working as a hospital doctor in order to brush up my skills. And I can't tell you how many meetings I've spoken at.'

'Did you have any time off?' the surprised woman asked.

'Yes,' Helen said, 'I did. In fact my leave ended with a lovely holiday and I'm feeling so much the better for it.'

Later that evening, as she stood on deck looking far out to sea, Helen thought about the future. She was longing to get back to the Congo, to Nebobongo and her friends there. But ... but the Congo was to be declared an independent country in just six weeks time, and independence often brought problems. Sometimes it brought violence, especially against white people.

'I'm glad my friends in Britain know about all this,' thought Helen. 'They'll be praying about it.'

* * *

'Hallelujah! Hallelujah! Praise the Lord God on high!'

Helen could hear the singing at Ibambi before she was within sight of the place. The talking drums had taken the message ahead of her and students, school children, nurses, workmen and many others couldn't contain their joy until she came! Then there was Nebobongo, dear Nebo. How Helen smiled when she remembered her unwillingness to move there in the first place!

'Welcome home!' her friends shouted. 'Welcome back to Nebo!'

Singing surrounded her. Children laughed and danced and clapped their hands in celebration. There is nothing like an African village celebrating. It's as though the very ground beats in time to the music.

'Look at the new buildings,' people said, pointing in several directions.

Helen's eyes opened wide. 'I see them!' she laughed. 'You have been busy. And they have proper roofs too! What a huge amount of work you've done while I've been away.'

But behind all the joy, all the laughing, all the dancing and singing, there was a trickle of fear. Independence was just two weeks away.

* * *

'There's a meeting being held at the dispensary this evening,' Helen was warned. 'I don't know what will come out of it.'

She didn't have long to wait.

'Will you come and join us at the meeting?' Helen was asked, although it wasn't so much an invitation as an order.

She went.

'We want to appoint a Congolese leader of the hospital,' she was told. 'Everywhere else has done that. We want you to make John Mangadima the Director.'

There was a silence while Helen prayed about what she should answer, a silence broken by John himself.

'I don't mind being in charge of the nurses and the administration work, but I couldn't ever be in charge of the hospital's medical work,' he said.

There was a noise like a bicycle tyre deflating as all those present, who had held their breath to see what would happen, relaxed and breathed out. A good compromise had been worked out without any argument at all. The Congolese workers had their Congolese Director, a fine Christian man who was content to leave medical decisions to the white lady doctor. When Helen thought about it later, she realised that they were entering different times in the Congo, new and uncertain times.

* * *

Morning dawned on 30th June, but it did not follow a night of sound sleep for many in the Congo, black or white. The nationals were so excited at the prospect of running their own country and many whites were fearful of what it would mean for them. In Nebobongo it was a day of praise and prayer.

'Mayaribu is coming!' the news travelled around. The headman of the region was making a formal visit.

'Look at them,' thought Helen. 'They are so pleased and proud. No wonder they are dressed is such bright colours!'

'Friends,' Mayaribu said to Helen and the three white missionaries who were visiting her, 'you are strangers among us but you are welcome to stay in our newly independent land.'

Murmurs of approval came from every direction and a sense of relief filled the missionaries. They had been accepted.

* * *

'Uhuru!' called the nurses when they saw Helen. 'Freedom!'

But the smiles that went with the greeting showed that they didn't want to be free of Helen!

'It's amazing,' the missionaries said to each other when they had time to talk. 'It seems that independence has come without bloodshed. How thankful we should be for that.'

But news from Leopoldville, the capital city, was not so good a short time later.

'There's been a mutiny in the army,' the news went round in whispers. 'And white families are leaving and going back to Europe.'

People listened to their radios and passed on any news they heard, most of it bad.

'Some white people have been attacked,' one said to the other. 'Terrible things are happening.'

'You don't think they'll happen here in Nebobongo?' his friend asked.

'No, of course not,' was the confident reply. Then that confidence melted away. 'At least I hope not. I really hope not.'

'We need to pray,' a young nurse said to Helen, as they worked together in the hospital.

'I am praying,' she assured her. 'We're all praying, how we're praying.'

* * *

'All missionaries have been called to a meeting at Ibambi,' Helen explained to John in mid July. 'You'll have to look after things while we are there.'

John looked at the doctor seriously.

'Of course I will,' he told her. 'The situation is getting really dangerous for you white people. I'm so sorry.'

Around twenty white missionaries met together at Ibambi. They had come from mission stations all around the area.

'What's happening where you are?' each asked the other, and waited anxiously for the replies.

'We've not been threatened at Nebobongo,' Helen said. 'At the moment things are all right there.'

'It's very tense where we are. Some people obviously would like us to leave.'

'A number of our workmen have left. They won't work under a white person now.'

Helen thought of John Mangadima and thanked God for his friendship and support.

At the end of the discussion missionaries were asked to write their names on a list if they wanted to be taken out of the Congo.

'How many have signed?' Helen enquired.

'Fifteen.'

She did not.

'We don't want to leave for good,' some told her. 'We just want to go over the border until things settle down here and it's safe to come back.'

Helen went back to Nebobongo alone.

'What happened?' asked John when she returned.

Helen explained.

'Why did you not sign? Why have you come back?'

His friend explained that she believed God meant her to stay, that she had work to do in the hospital. John looked deep into her eyes with a look that spoke right to Helen's heart. It said 'thank you' in a way that he could not put into words. But even in his look of gratitude there was fear for the future.

* * *

'What's happening?' one of the nurses asked later that evening.

'It's a truck-full of soldiers,' was the reply. 'But they've driven right through.'

The air was very tense when Helen headed for bed. Each time she heard a rat in the roof space she jumped, thinking it was someone breaking into her house.

Knock! Knock!

'The soldiers have come back for me!' Helen shook at the thought.

She had just been praying for someone to come to stay with her so that she would not be alone in the house. But she hadn't meant soldiers! Fear made her heart beat so hard that it felt as though it would burst.

'Who's there?' she asked fearfully before opening the door.

'We are,' said two women's voices. 'It's Mama Taadi and Mama Damaris.'

Helen opened the door and hugged her friends as they came in.

'God wakened us both up,' they explained, 'each in our own houses. And he told us to come and sleep in your house so that you won't be here alone.'

'Praise the Lord!' breathed Helen. 'He has answered my prayer.'

The three women set about making up beds and then they settled down to a hot drink before reading *Daily Light* and going off to bed.

* * *

'It's been decided that we should come and stay here with you until the trouble dies down,' two lady missionaries from forty miles away said, when they arrived at Nebobongo the next day.

'God is so good,' smiled Helen. 'That means Mama Taadi and Mama Damaris will be able to sleep in peace in their own homes.'

She explained to her visitors what had happened the previous night. In the four weeks that followed the three women worked together and things seemed to be settling down. Rumours of awful things were heard from time to time, but they were still made to feel welcome in Nebobongo. Their Congolese friends, at least, didn't want them out of the country. In fact, things seemed so much better that most of the missionaries who had signed the list and left came back into the Congo again.

'I'll have my nurse back working with me!' thought Helen delightedly. 'I've missed her such a lot.'

But when the evacuees returned, her nurse did not.

* * *

'The sound of a truck puts my mind in a spin,' Helen confided in John one day.

'I know what you mean,' he said. 'Sometimes it's a truckload of soldiers, and you never know what's going to happen when they come. And other times it's a truck bringing people who are so ill that hardly anything can be done for them.'

'That's because most hospitals in the region have no doctor and people are being brought huge distances to Nebobongo. These are terrible days.'

John agreed. Looking at Helen, he realised that she was utterly exhausted. And the doctor, as she looked at her dear Congolese friend, knew that he was every bit as tired as she was. When the new government instructed Helen to work two days a week at Wamba, sixty miles from Nebobongo, John wondered how she would cope. It wasn't just the extra work that worried him, but also the dangers to a white woman travelling along country roads. He went with her whenever he could.

* * *

'Do not go any further,' they were told, when they were flagged down one day six miles from Wamba. Thankfully John Mangadima was with her on this occasion.

'What's wrong?' he asked.

'The white people at Wamba have all been tied up. You should not go there,' they told Helen.

'But I must go,' she insisted. 'I have patients in Wamba who need a doctor.'

'I am coming with you,' John told her firmly, and would not listen to her arguments against it.

Just before Wamba they were stopped again, this time by a nasty looking bunch of rebel soldiers.

'Get out of your car!' they ordered Helen.

John was first out.

'Do not touch her!' he said firmly. 'She is one of us. She is our doctor.'

The men moved away from the car and eventually Helen and John were allowed to go to the hospital. But on arrival they discovered that all the nurses and most of the patients had left as things had turned very ugly earlier in the day. There was nothing for it but to turn the car and go right back to Nebobongo.

'There's a road block ahead,' Helen said, as they drove along. 'We're in for more hassle, I'm afraid.'

But when their car reached the road block, the soldiers clicked their heels together, saluted and let them right through!

'Praise the Lord!' said Helen from her heart. 'I think they took you at your word this morning, John, that I am one of you. Thank you.'

* * *

A year of uncertainty passed from Independence Day and its anniversary drew near. For several years there had been a youth group called Campaigners in Nebobongo, and it was decided to take all the young people, about ninety of them, to Ibambi for the day.

'We'll set off first thing to march the seven miles before it gets too hot.'

Dressed in their Campaigner uniforms, and with their flags flying high, they all set off.

'What singing!' Helen thought. 'Where do they get the energy to sing and march at the same time?'

She was feeling unusually tired and not really very well as they marched. After a great day together Helen was more than happy to accept a lift back to Nebobongo.

'That's not like the doctor,' several people said, when they saw her returning home by car.

And it was not like her at all. Helen was coming down with an illness and it was more than three months before she was able to work again. But work was not easy, especially because there were so many shortages.

'She really does love us,' one of Helen's nurses said one day. 'Despite all the shortages and all the difficulties, and all the arguments she does everything she possibly can to help our people.'

Her friend agreed. 'There seems to be no end of trouble,' he added. 'It just goes on month after month after month.'

What he said was true. As the months passed, life for Helen was just one challenge after another. But she continued to do what God had put in her heart to do, to serve the people of the Congo, and to serve them in his love despite all the difficulties she met. Months became years and the work went on.

* * *

'There has been a rebellion in the northeast province,' the voice said on the radio, and the news travelled throughout Nebobongo like wildfire.

'What bad timing!' complained Helen, who was about to drive a thousand miles to Kampala in Uganda to collect much-needed medical supplies, petrol and food. 'I'd best wait to let this settle down.'

John agreed, thinking it was very good timing. The doctor might already have left and her life could have been in danger. He was glad to have her safely at Nebobongo. But Nebo wasn't safe. On 15th August 1964 a truck load of soldiers drove to the hospital. 'Treat this man,' they demanded, as they hauled an injured civilian from their truck.

Helen hoped that they would then move on and leave them in peace. But they did not. The soldiers remained and occupied Nebobongo for the next five months!

* * *

'There was a murder in one of the nearby villages,' someone whispered to Helen in the ward one day.

'Shh,' she said. 'I heard. Or maybe this is another one.'

News of attacks and murders and other dreadful things reached Helen nearly every day.

'Wamba's been taken by the rebel army,' was hot news. Then it was Paulis that was taken.

'They're getting nearer,' John warned.

Army trucks went along the road so often, but Helen never grew used to them. Each one spelled Danger with a capital D.

'Will the awful things we hear about elsewhere happen in Nebobongo?' she wondered.

Some fears were spoken about, others were not. Fear was so real that people felt that if they were to stretch out their hands they would touch it.

'Don't speak about the troubles when you are in the wards,' John told the nurse. 'I think there are spies among the patients, especially the men. Be very careful indeed.'

'But are there spies among the nurses too?' he wondered. He did not know.

'How long will this go on?' Helen asked herself.

And from time to time her mind went back to when she became a Christian. It was a long time ago, but it was fresh in her mind. Dr Scroggie had spoken wise words to her. What were they? She had no trouble remembering. 'Knowing Jesus is just the beginning, and there's a long journey ahead. My prayer for you is that you will go on through the years to know his power. And it is perhaps in God's plan for you to suffer for your Saviour as he suffered for you.'

* * *

Helen's day of suffering did come. Things too terrible to tell happened to her at the hands of Congolese rebel soldiers, things so horrible and shocking that she wished she were dead. In a way that we cannot understand they were part of God's plan for her and she knew that, even at the time. With her body battered and broken and her back teeth kicked out, Helen survived when others did not. But she survived to endure further months of terror. It was only afterwards that Helen and those who were with her at that time discovered what had happened.

The National Army did not have enough soldiers to beat the rebel soldiers. To increase their numbers they paid white South Africans, among others, to join the National Army. When rebel soldiers were shot and killed by these white men, their fellow rebels went into panic mode. They had been told by witchdoctors that white men could not harm them, yet here were white men killing them! Deciding that they must be using very powerful witchcraft, they did awful things to the people they captured, Helen and many other missionaries among them. It would do no good to describe the things that happened. It is enough to say that they were kept as prisoners and treated cruelly for five long months before help came and they were released.

Days after their release, Helen and some of the other British missionaries flew home.

'It's snowing,' thought Helen, as she looked out the aeroplane window when it came in to land.

Was it a dream? No, she must be home. It didn't snow in the Congo!

* * *

'Mother,' Helen said, when she was able to telephone home. 'Mother, it's me, Helen.'

For Mrs Roseveare a miracle had happened. Some weeks earlier she had read in the newspaper the headline, 'Doctor Killed in Ibambi.' Knowing of no other doctor in the area except Helen, Mrs Roseveare's heart broke. When the captives were eventually released someone from *The Daily Telegraph* phoned Mrs Roseveare from Leopoldville to tell her that Helen was among those who had been set free. Within days she was back home in England. So it was that New Year 1965 started in the best possible way for the Roseveares. Helen, although deeply shocked and in need of many months of love to help her to begin to recover, was home. And her mother had her daughter back from the dead.

'You build, I teach'

It was not easy for Helen Roseveare to decide to return to the Congo (now renamed Zaire) after fifteen months at home. For a very long time bad dreams troubled her sleep and horrid memories haunted her days.

But God still had work for her to do in Africa and he led her back there in March 1966. Travelling with another returning missionary, they sailed to Mombasa and then headed for central Africa.

'From the stifling heat of Mombasa we started on the long climb to the cool of Nairobi, 5,500 feet above sea level,' Helen wrote. 'Up again, to 8,000 feet; through the Rift valley with its magnificent views; up yet again, to 9,000 feet, and then across the hills and down the long slope to Lake Victoria and Kampala in Uganda.'

Africa at its beautiful best welcomed her back.

'All along the route smiling villagers and happy schoolchildren waved to us. Herds of wild elephants and wildebeest, wart-hogs and antelope grazed in the surrounding grasslands.'

But what lay ahead? Helen wondered. Would she be welcomed back? Would her Zairian friends think she should have come back sooner, that she had abandoned them? She travelled on not knowing quite what to expect.

* * *

It was 8.30 on the morning of Easter Sunday when Helen reached Nebobongo. If she still had fears about whether or not she'd be welcomed, they must have melted in the morning sun. Mama Taadi was there to throw her arms round her old friend, as was Mama Damaris. John Mangadima let the women say their hellos first then came forward with tears in his eyes and an enormous smile on his face. Orphans showered Helen with kisses, and the children of the nurses, teachers and workmen did the same. Patients from the nearby leprosy camp, some with crutches, others struggling to walk, came up the hill to present her with huge armfuls of blossom. Helen's nurses sang their welcome and the midwives and workmen joined in.

From Nebobongo Helen went to Ibambi, arriving just as the Easter congregation of about 3,000 people was leaving the church. Then Pastor Ndugu, who had been as a father to her, came out of the crowd with his wife and their tearful wordless welcome said everything Helen needed to hear. Was she welcome back? Yes, a thousand times yes! Was she still loved? Yes, ten thousand times yes! Their child was home again. Back into the church they went and sang their praises to God for his goodness. Later, as the crowds thinned, Helen found the answer to her last question. Did God still have work for her to do in Zaire? Looking round she saw poverty and the ill-health that comes from it. Men, no longer able to afford to buy trousers, just had loincloths wrapped round themselves. Gone were the bright frocks the women had worn; many were dressed in grass skirts instead. That was bad enough, but what hurt Helen much more were the swollen stomachs of hungry children, men's ribs sticking out so much they could be counted, children with painfully thin legs and people of all ages bearing the marks of brutality. Limbs were missing and scars marked many arms, legs and bodies. If ever a doctor was needed, Helen was. The civil war had left Zaire a broken country.

'The schools that are still open have no equipment,' she wrote home. 'Hospital and clinic buildings are pock-marked with hundreds of bullet holes and totally empty of anything useful. There is no medical equipment and there are no medicines. Instead of all that was here before there is devastation, total devastation. The country is in melt-down. I don't know where we should begin.'

Helen didn't know where to begin, but Dr Becker, who was based in Nyankunde, had a vision he wanted to share with her.

'This area measures 500 square miles. If we were to build up the work in Nyankunde we could serve that whole area,' said Dr Becker.

Helen nodded. 'We would need a big hospital.'
'I reckon 250 beds.'

'And outpatients?' said Helen.

'We should aim to treat 1000 a day,' Dr Becker told her.

He had obviously done some serious thinking.

The two doctors talked and talked, leaving Helen's head spinning as she thought it through afterwards.

'What a vision!' she said to herself. 'We would have medical and surgical facilities, maternity and children's wards, a place for people with leprosy, a dispensary, a school for training nurses – the full three year course!'

Her heart raced at the prospect.

'We would have another school for training girls as midwives and even small rural hospitals – up to twelve of them – staffed from Nyankunde.'

Dr Becker and Helen had active imaginations!

* * *

On the nineteen-hour long journey back to Nebobongo Helen hit hard reality.

Yes, the Nyankunde project was the best way forward in the long term, but would her dear friends back in Ibambi and Nebo understand that? She was not sure. For a week the elders talked about it with heavy hearts.

'Our doctor is not long back and now she wants to go away,' some said.

Helen tried to explain she didn't WANT to go away; God seemed to be leading her to Nyankunde.

'Our young men will no longer be able to train as nurses,' moaned others.

'Yes, they will,' insisted Helen. 'If they come to Nyankunde and do the three years' training they will get a government certificate. Then they'll be able to work anywhere, even here in Nebobongo. It will be a much better training than the one we are able to do here.'

'Do we not need a doctor as much as the people at Nyankunde who already have Dr Becker?'

'Yes, of course you do,' Helen admitted, 'and a doctor will come regularly.'

Her friends shook their heads doubtfully.

'Remember,' she said, 'a doctor can come in by small aircraft if you cut an airstrip for him to land.'

At last there was a glimmer of light in their eyes. And by the end of the week the elders and the mission council had agreed to let their beloved doctor move to Nyankunde. But Helen saw that the sparkle had gone out of their eyes and their steps had slowed down with sadness. Her heart was in turmoil.

However, the vision for Nyankunde was what God had put in her mind and she was sure that was the direction in which he was leading her to go. So it was very soon after their joyful welcome to Doctor Helen Roseveare that the people of Ibambi and Nebobongo wished her a sad and tearful goodbye.

* * *

Government permission was needed to open the hospital and nurses' training school in Nyankunde. A whole book could be written about all the ins and outs of how that happened. But nobody would read it because it would be all about filling in forms then filling them in again, just before filling them in for a third time, and a fourth! To Helen, who thought quickly and did things quickly, everything seemed to move SO slowly. However, the time came when four classes, each of twelve students, were chosen for nurses' training, all of them young men. Among them were those students whose training at Nebobongo had been brought to a halt by the rebellion.

The great Nyankunde vision was becoming hard facts and careful plans. Dr Becker would be in charge of the whole hospital and Helen was to be responsible for nursing training. Of course, there would be coming and going between the two doctors as Helen's students would do their practical training in Dr Becker's hospital wards. After a long discussion about future plans Helen stood, early one morning, looking at her nursing school. She could see the building and knew exactly what it would look like inside: classrooms, all neatly laid out with students listening to lectures and watching demonstrations, blackboards covered with carefully-drawn diagrams, boxes of bandages for practising dressings and many other things besides. Then Helen grinned, shook herself, and looked ahead. What was actually in front of her was a plot of ground 4 or 5 acres in size, covered with brambles and elephant grass taller than she was! She grinned.

'That's what it will look like when it's finished and in use,' she said to herself. 'One day that vision will be a reality!'

* * *

'It won't just be a building,' Helen wrote home to a friend. 'Imagine this. National nurses, midwives and health workers, trained here in Nyankunde, will one day serve the whole north-eastern region of Zaire, all quarter of a million square miles of it.

Those who are trained here will not stay in Nyankunde; they will spread all over the region taking health care to where there is none at present.'

She looked up from the page as the vision almost dissolved before her very eyes, and then picked up her pen again.

'I can just see streams of refugees, hungry, naked and sick being cared for where they are. No longer will people have to travel many days to get help. Health care will be where they are. And more than that, my prayer is that our graduates will go out, not only as nurses, midwives and health workers, but as Christians. How wonderful it will be if they take the good news of Jesus Christ as well as good medicine to people who are sick in body and sin-sick in soul.'

Big things have small beginnings, Helen knew, and the small beginning of the nursing school was a camp table and a wooden chair at which she sat in the sun on the day her students were due to arrive. Twenty-two gathered that morning.

'What is your name?' Helen asked each one, ticking them off on her list of those who were expected. 'Please go to John Mangadima and he will give you all you need.'

John, who had come to be Assistant Director of the nursing school, handed out blankets, plates, mugs and spoons as well as lamps, matches and soap.

'Where exactly is the nursing school?' asked a would-be student, who looked as though he knew everything there was to know already!

Helen looked up from her sheet of paper and waved her arm vaguely in the direction of the brambles and elephant grass.

'Over there,' she said, trying to keep her voice steady.

'And the dormitories,' he went on. 'Where are the dormitories?'

Helen looked straight into his eyes.

'Over there too,' she said, in a tone that warned him that arguing was not a good idea.

* * *

John Mangadima and Helen busied themselves about all that had to be done as the truth dawned on the twenty two young men who had just arrived. What was going on in their minds could be seen reflected in their faces!

'There is no school!' one whispered to another.

'And I don't think there are dormitories for us to sleep in either,' his friend replied.

One wondered if it was a hoax. Had they been tricked into coming to a college that didn't exist?

'I will show you where you are sleeping,' John said, taking charge of the students. 'Most will be in two classrooms of the primary school. But, as there is not room for all of you there, a few will stay with the church elders or in missionaries' homes. I will call your names one by one and tell you where you are to go.'

John began calling the students' names.

'What's all this?' one student muttered. 'I don't want to live in a primary school. I've finished with primary school. I've been a year in secondary school.'

'This is insulting,' the young man next to him agreed. 'I would never have come if I'd thought it would be like this.'

Helen watched what was happening and listened to the mutterings and mumblings around her.

'Will this work?' she wondered. 'Will they be willing to do what we are going to ask them to do?'

She not only wondered, she also prayed ... hard.

* * *

That afternoon the students arrived back at Helen's table and chair, most in a mood of confusion and annoyance.

'Right,' said Helen, putting on her most encouraging voice, 'let's go.'

Twenty-two boys, along with John Mangadima, followed the doctor through sticky mud, between jagged brambles until they found themselves weaving their way among elephant grass that was so tall they were hidden from the rest of the world. The boys – most of them were between seventeen and twenty years old – began to enjoy the fun. By the time they reached the top of the little hill up which Helen led them, they were in much better humour.

'Phew,' thought Helen, as the boys laughed and joked between themselves. 'Thank you, Lord, for the change of mood.'

'Look down the valley,' she told the lads.

They turned and looked.

'That is our school,' she said, pointing to a green grassy area where there was not a building in sight, 'and those are your dormitories,' she said, pointing to another patch of land.

The boys stopped smiling. Some looked puzzled, others looked cross. A few looked insulted. Dr Helen Roseveare prayed hard and then appealed to them all, looking into the eyes of one young lad after another, 'You build,' she said. 'I teach.'

It was as though time stopped.

It was as though the world stopped.

Helen's suggestion certainly stopped twenty-two young men firmly in their tracks.

'This is what I'm asking you to do,' she explained, after what seemed like forever. 'I'm asking you to take your shirts off and become workmen.'

Shirts were a sign of importance in the students' eyes.

'I'm asking you to use workmen's tools to clear the ground of brambles and elephant grass. I'm asking you to go miles into the forest to fell trees and then haul them back here with no tractor to help you, just your own strong shoulders.'

The boys' eyes were opening wider with every sentence she spoke.

'I'm asking you to build dormitories for you to sleep in and a nursing school, doing everything including thatching the roofs. Then will you build houses in order that married students can have their families staying with them?'

Running out of breath, Helen drew to a halt … briefly.

'And, when you've done all that,' she told them, 'then I'll teach you.'

Standing tall, for she needed the young men to be able to picture her as their teacher, Helen went on. 'I'll teach you everything you need to know to be nurses and health workers, every single thing.'

Twenty two black faces searched her white face for answers.

'Are you being serious? Do you really expect us to take off our shirts and be workmen? Do you think we came here to haul trees through the forest? Who do you think we are?'

'You build, I teach,' Helen repeated.

Some boys closed their eyes and shook their heads as if they were trying to wake up out of a bad dream. Others just stood and stared at Helen and then down the hill at the ground where the school could be.

'You build, I teach.'

One or two students looked surly, insulted at the suggestion Helen had laid before them.

'We'll meet tomorrow at 6.30 am,' the doctor told them. 'You can tell me your decision then.'

* * *

That evening a service of welcome had been arranged for the boys and all of them attended.

'I don't see why we should go,' a number of them complained to the others.

'Because there's nothing else to do here,' a sensible lad said. 'We might as well go to see what they have to say for themselves.'

Helen struggled during the service as she tried to keep her mind on the Lord and his Word. It was so easy to be distracted by some of the lads whose faces made them look like cats whose cream had been taken away. But, as the service went on, some of the young men's hearts seemed to soften just a little bit.

'Lord,' Helen prayed, before she went to bed, 'if these are the students you want me to teach, please make them willing to do all that needs to be done.'

* * *

It was 6.30 am and raining. Not the kind of rain that lashes down and then goes off, but the kind that keeps falling, soaks you through and makes the world look misty. Helen put up her folding table, took out her wooden chair and sat down to read her Bible and to wait for the boys to come … or not.

'They're an hour late,' she thought, when she looked at her watch and saw it was 7.30 am.

The hour that followed seemed to last very much longer than sixty minutes because each minute seem longer than sixty seconds.

'It's half past eight,' said Helen to herself, having had a sideways glance at her watch in case she was within sight of any of the lads. She certainly didn't want them to think she was being impatient.

'Good morning,' a soaking wet Helen said briskly at 8.45 am to the twenty two young men who appeared in front of her.

Not a word was said about them being late, or about them knowing quite well that she had been sitting in the rain for two-and-a-quarter hours! They boys sat down and Helen told them that they were going to sing a hymn before having a short Bible study. As they sang together she could see the relief on their faces. They'd made their point by being late. They were not particularly happy about what they had to do, but they would go along with it.

* * *

'We'll divide into three groups,' Helen told the lads when their Bible study was over, 'and each group will appoint its own leader.'

That was done and the three leaders immediately felt a sense of importance.

'Now,' went on Helen, 'here are axes to take into the forest to begin to fell the trees we'll need.'

The leader of the first group handed out the axes.

'Group two, you'll each take a hoe and start clearing the land where the dormitory will be built. And group three, will you take the scythes to cut down the long grass next to the dormitory site?'

'What are we going to build?' a boy asked.

Helen smiled. 'I think that's where we'll put the football pitch and ...'

A smile lit up their faces!

'... and the food garden beyond that.'

The work had begun. And Helen knew that she'd won the boys over when one of them looked her in the eye and said, 'O.K. You win – we build and you teach!'

The Miracle of Nyankunde

'This is hard work!' was a complaint often heard in the weeks that followed. If it was said in a joking way, Helen would smile and say that they wouldn't really know what hard work was until she started teaching them! If it was said seriously, she was as encouraging as she could be. She couldn't risk them walking out on her. If the boys were honest, they realised that the doctor never asked them to do what she would not do herself. She too had blisters on her hands from chopping down trees, digging and hoeing.

'When the first house is finished we'll have a celebration,' Helen told the boys, who needed to celebrate from time to time to keep them going.

'Let's have a football match,' one of them suggested.

As soon as the roof was completed on the first house, the demands for a football match were so noisy that work was abandoned for the afternoon.

'They deserve it,' Helen commented to Dr Becker, who had come to see the fun and games.

'I know they do,' he agreed. 'But you're grudging every moment of it because you want them to get on with the work,' he added kindly.

Ouch!

* * *

'You said that some students were coming from Nebobongo,' one of the young men said to Helen. 'Why are they not here helping with the building? Are they going to wait until all the hard work is done and then just arrive to start classes?'

That was a fair point, and Helen knew it, though she tried to explain what terrible times the Nebobongo students had had during the civil war and that some of their number had even been killed.

'When will our lessons begin?' was a demand that was heard more and more often as the weeks went past.

'We hope to begin on 1st October,' was Helen's hopeful suggestion.

That might have been possible had several students not taken malaria and then dysentery, and had all of the others not been really, really tired. The 1st October came and went with the hope that at the end of the month a start might be possible.

* * *

'See how well it's all developing,' Helen encouraged her workers. 'We're nearly there. Just another week or two and we'll be finished. I think it's time for me to ask the tailor to start making your nursing uniforms. Don't you?'

That was enough encouragement to keep them going for one more day. Helen had to find encouragement after encouragement day after day to keep the lads at it. At least nobody complained about not sleeping at night. They all went to bed, herself included, absolutely exhausted!

* * *

'We need a flagpole to finish it off,' Helen announced, towards the end of October 1966. 'Let's make it as high as is safe.'

A tall straight tree was cut down and the branches hacked off. Then the trunk was made as smooth as possible.

'Let's measure it before we sink it in the ground,' someone suggested.

Several of the lads stepped out along the length of the pole.

'It's forty-nine feet long,' one shouted.

'No it's not! Your feet are too small. It's forty seven feet long.'

The flagpole, which was actually forty-eight feet long, was erected in the centre of the compound. Frustration and irritation began to change into excitement and anticipation. The tailor had all the uniforms ready. All that was missing were the students from Nebobongo.

* * *

Three long months after arriving at Nyankunde the young men, dressed in their smart new uniforms, gathered to ask God's blessing on the new school of nursing. It was Doctor Becker who led in prayer and John Mangadima who pulled the flag slowly to the top of the flagpole as everyone sang the Zairian national anthem. With a final tug, John released the flag which caught what little wind there was and opened against the sky. Helen and the other members of staff felt lumps in their throats and the beginnings of tears in their eyes. How good God had been to them! When that moment was over the students - there were thirty six of them by then - abandoned all seriousness and became fanatical footballers in a match that helped them to celebrate in the way they enjoyed best – kicking a poor unsuspecting football around the pitch they had made with their very own hands!

* * *

One week of lectures later, the boys realised that they might not get blisters on their hands from studying nursing, but it was still going to be very hard work indeed. That was when it happened. The Nyankunde compound filled with so much noise that it sounded as though it might explode. A truck had driven in, thick with mud far up its sides, and filled with people. Helen rushed to the front of the crowd. Could it be? Was it possible? Had the truck come from Nebobongo? She searched the passengers for familiar faces … and found them. Thinner than before, bashed, bruised, dirty and tired, some of them ill, but they were there! Her long-awaited students had come with their wives and children! The nursing school was complete!

The boys who had spent three months building at Nyankunde joined in the excitement. They could see for themselves that the newcomers had been through hard times. In any case, the college was complete; it was just time to get on with the business of training to be nurses. To Helen's great delight her friend Basuana from Nebobongo arrived with the students. If anyone could keep things in good order it was Basuana. A wave of relief and excitement passed through Helen like a bolt of electricity. This unlikely, amazing, wonderful project WAS going to work. God had brought everything and everyone together. He was in control.

* * *

'How do you spend your days now that the nursing school is up and running?' a friend wrote to Helen.

'I'll describe a typical day for you,' she began her reply. 'My day lasts from 5 am until after midnight. It begins with coffee and my quiet time with God, then breakfast. At 6.30 everyone meets for morning prayers and classes start right afterwards. We give twelve lectures every day, four to each of the three classes. With meal breaks and staff meetings, that takes us to just before 9 pm when we meet for evening prayers, after which the generator is switched off and Nyankunde drifts off into darkness.'

Helen smiled at the thought of her friend reading the letter and thinking the next sentence would go on to say that she then went to bed and slept soundly for the night.

'That's when I light my little lantern and get down to work,'she continued. 'Usually I begin by marking the students'books. Then it's down to preparing the next day's lectures.'

Standing up for a minute to stretch her weary limbs, she wondered how best to describe the process of preparing lectures.

'I think it would be easier for you to understand if I made a list of the process,' she wrote. 'So here goes.'

1. I read up about the subjects that are going to be taught.
2. I take notes and work out the teaching points.
3. I write out my lessons.
4. I translate them into French.
5. I make stencils of the notes on my trusty typewriter.
6. I duplicate the notes for the students.

'The seventh is that I thank the Lord for the day, ask his blessing on the night, and collapse in a heap in bed. That's usually about one o'clock in the morning.'

When Helen's friend received the letter and read it, she wondered how her friend kept going on just four or five hours sleep a night. Helen Roseveare often wondered that too!

* * *

During her years in Nebobongo, Helen had taught in Swahili, and eventually she used the language well. When the Congo became Zaire at Independence, the new government decided that French should be used in secondary schools, colleges and universities. Having spoken Swahili for so many years, Helen found it difficult to work in French and preparing her lectures took a very long time. It was also difficult for the students, many of whom spoke Swahili, or one of the other languages used in Zaire, in their own homes.

* * *

'Now we're getting what we came for,' one student said to another, some weeks into the course.

His friend nodded his head. 'It's very hard work. My brain feels tired after every lecture.'

'I know. I'm the same. But I was thinking one day that she is just doing what she said she would do.'

'What was that?' his fellow student asked.

'She said that clearing the ground and putting up buildings would be hard work. But that when all the work was done she would work hard and teach us everything we needed to know to be nurses.'

'That's true,' replied the young Zairian. 'When we were working on the buildings the doctor worked hard to keep up with us and now we are having to work hard to keep up with all she is teaching us.'

* * *

Now that the students were doing what they had come to do at Nyankunde, any construction work had to be done by workmen rather than nursing students.

'How many men will you need to build the new classroom block?' Helen asked Basuana.

'I think twenty four men will be enough,' he replied.

The men were employed and the work got underway. As the walls of the big building went up, Helen's students tried to guess what each room would be used for. They even offered to help with the building work on Saturdays! It was on a Thursday evening in January 1969 that Basuana came to Helen with a problem.

'The building is so large that my workmen are not able to put the roof on. We need someone who knows what he's doing for that job. Will I tell the workmen we don't need them? There's no point of them just hanging around doing nothing until we find a roofer.

Basuana and Helen knew each other very well,

and they both believed that God knew they needed a roofer.

'No,' they decided in faith. 'We'll not send the men away.'

The following morning, when Helen was going down to have prayers with the workmen, she passed a young American on the way.

'Good morning,' she said.

The man looked at her and nodded.

'Poor soul,' thought Helen. 'From the sight of him I don't think he had any sleep last night. I wonder what's wrong.'

Suddenly, out of nowhere, Basuana appeared.

'Do you know who the man is that you passed on the hill?' he asked.

Helen shook her head. 'No, I don't know who he is.'

Her friend couldn't contain his excitement.

'He's a roofer!'

No sooner did Helen hear the words than she was off up the hill after him. The young man, being tired, had not gone too far.

'Sir!' she called out, as she caught up on him.

'Please stop and let me explain who I am and what I want to talk to you about.'

Helen poured out the whole story about the teaching block being complete apart from the roof, and how the roof was so large that it needed a roofer to oversee the work being done. Hardly able to keep his eyes open, the young man then explained why he was in Nyankunde.

'My wife was flown here yesterday for urgent medical treatment and I drove through the night to be with her. She'll be here for some time and I'm more than willing to help you in any way I can. But, please can I get some sleep first. I'm utterly exhausted.'

By the time the American's wife was well enough to go home the roof was on the teaching block.

'God knew exactly when we needed him,' said Basuana.

Helen smiled.

* * *

When the buildings were completed and the nursing course had been running for some time, government inspectors came to see that everything was up to standard. For days they went around the place listening to lectures, watching students, measuring walls, looking in cupboards, reading students' notes, questioning Helen … the list went on and on and on. On the Saturday Helen and a colleague took the two inspectors for a picnic at Lake Albert. They had a relaxing time together, the first time that week that anyone had had a chance to relax.

'Goodness me!' Helen laughed, when they arrived back at Nyankunde. 'I didn't realise we were so popular!'

The students had rushed out to meet Helen and

her friend on their return.

'Did you succeed?' they asked. 'Were you successful?'

Helen and the other women looked at each other, not having a clue what they were being asked.

'You took the inspectors away to Lake Albert for the day. Did you succeed?'

Still Helen was totally confused.

'Start from the beginning and explain what you mean,' she said, when they had calmed down enough for her to he heard.

One of the students took on the job of explaining what he thought was obvious to his seriously silly teachers.

'You took the two inspectors away to Lake Albert to put them in a good mood and offer them a bribe so that the nursing school will get the government stamp. Did they accept the bribe?'

Helen and her colleague could hardly believe what they were nearing.

'No, of course we didn't offer them a bribe,' Helen answered, horrified at the very thought. 'The buildings are good. The teaching is good. We don't need to offer them a bribe.'

The students shook their heads in despair. These white doctors might be very clever and know all about medicine, but they didn't seem to know anything about life.

* * *

It took a very, very long time for the Zairian government to recognise the college at Nyankunde, and the students were probably right in thinking that a bribe would have allowed it to happen quicker. But Helen and her Christian friends would never have stooped to that. Instead, they had to be patient (most of the time) and wait ... and wait. One day, more than two years later, news arrived at Nyankunde that the nursing school was about to get the government stamp of approval. Not only that, but it would give the nurses a monthly pay cheque!

'Praise the Lord!' was probably the expression that was heard most often in the hospital that day.

A few nights later, after she had finished her long day's work, Helen sat down to write a letter to all those who had sent money to the nursing school. Christians in several different countries had kept the place going since its beginning.

'The government is going to pay one third of all our costs in the future,' she wrote, 'and when they are able to afford it, they'll take over the whole budget.'

Two things happened in the weeks that followed. Several people who had been sending money regularly stopped doing so as they thought it was no longer needed, and the government decided not to pay the money! The next few months were difficult as there was only just enough to pay the workers and nothing else. Helen, who had been ill for a time, went back to England to recover. On her return to Nyankunde, just four days before her students came back for the new term, and when money was needed to meet all their expenses, Helen started to open her large pile of letters.

'What's this one?' she asked herself, when she saw the headed notepaper. 'Oh, it's from the education authority. I wonder what they want.'

She read the letter through, her eyes opening wide as she did so.

'They're giving us £1,500,' Helen said softly. 'Giving ....'

She reread the letter, daring to hope it was true.

'They ARE giving us £1,500!' she laughed. 'Praise the Lord! Never in the history of Nyankunde have we needed £1,500 more than we do today!'

With that money in the bank, the work of training nurses to serve the people who lived in a quarter of a million square miles of Zaire went on. Dr Becker's and Helen's vision was becoming a reality.

* * *

By 1972 Helen knew in her heart that the time had come for her to leave Nyankunde. Soon afterwards she heard news of the death of Jack Scholes, the senior missionary who had welcomed her to the Congo all those years ago. Helen was able to go to his funeral where there was sadness mixed with great rejoicing that God had taken Jack home to be with him in heaven. It seemed to Helen to be the end of an era. But a new era was beginning, as John Mangadima was appointed as Assistant Medical Director at Nebobongo.

* * *

'What are you doing?' John asked when Helen arrived one day in his office at Nebo.

'I'm collecting some facts and figures to tell the people back home what's being done here.'

John leant over her shoulder and read what she had written.

'372 major operations were carried out in 1972 with only six deaths among them.'

'Oh Doctor,' John Mangadima smiled. 'Don't bother with things like that. Just tell them that nearly 200 people asked the Lord to be their Saviour through the medical services here last year.'

Helen turned round and hugged John hard. He understood.

* * *

When the time came for Helen to leave for England many kind things were said. But Nyelongo, one of the workmen, best captured what she had come to mean to the Zairian people. He stood up in front of the huge crowd that had gathered to say farewell and told a story. 'Years ago, when we were building the teaching block, I was late for work one day. You had already gone into the school and I was scared I would be in trouble. But when you came out you didn't give me a row. Instead you asked how my baby was. I didn't know you even knew I had a baby. "My baby is very sick," I said, and you asked where it was. I said the baby was at home. "Why is the baby not in hospital?" you asked. I explained that I didn't have money to bring the baby to hospital. You were so angry!'

Everyone was listening to Nyelongo's story and wondering what happened next.

'You rushed to the Land Rover and ordered me to get in and then drove all the way to my village. I'd never been in a car before! When we got to my home and you saw our baby you ordered my wife into the car along with the baby and took us all back to the hospital.'

Some people in the crowd remembered this and nodded their heads.

'But I was worried,' went on Nyelongo. 'I thought money would be taken from my pay at the end of the month to cover the cost of my baby being in hospital. But when the end of the month came, no money had been taken off. When I discovered all my money was there I rushed to my wife and said to her, "Look! All my money is here. Now I know that what the Doctor and Basuana say about the love of God is true.'

Helen's eyes were filling up with tears as the

story went on. But Nyelongo had kept the very best bit to the end.

'That day my wife and I asked the Lord Jesus to be our Saviour and we have followed him every day since.'

Passport Please

'You must be glad to be back home in England,' a friend said to Helen soon after her return. 'I can imagine you settling down to a nice quiet job as a country doctor. That would do you good after your busy life in Zaire.'

The thought of a nice quiet life horrified Helen! In any case, she had a suspicion that a country doctor did more work than her friend thought.

'I don't think so,' she replied. 'I believe that the Lord will have work to keep me busy until the day he takes me home to heaven.'

Far from settling down somewhere in the English countryside, Helen soon found herself travelling the world speaking at large and small meetings of people, most of whom were interested in missions.

* * *

In November 1976, Helen was invited to speak at a huge missionary conference in America. 'There will be over 17,000 students there,' she was told.

Helen shook in her shoes!

'As well as the students there will be people from over a hundred missionary organisations. Our speakers are known world-wide.'

The thought of standing up in front of that number of people scared her stiff. In any case, she didn't think she was well-known enough to be invited!

'The main speaker is also from England,' she was told. For the first time in the conversation she relaxed. The other English speaker was Rev. John Stott whom Helen knew and admired.

'How do you speak to over 17,000 people?' Helen asked Mr Stott, when they were together at the conference.

That wise man turned to her, smiled, and said, 'Don't look at 17,000 faces. Just look at one person in the very front row. All the others are just copies of that one!'

With that good advice in her mind, Helen stood in front of the huge gathering and spoke to everyone there as though there was just one person in the hall. Dr Billy Graham, the most famous preacher in the whole world at that time, was also speaking at the conference. Helen was looking forward to hearing what he had to say from God's Word. She sat right at the front with paper and a pencil to take notes on Dr Graham's talk had to say. But so relieved was she that her talk was over that she fell sound asleep and didn't hear a single word of his talk!

* * *

The following summer Helen was invited to be with young people again, but not 17,000 of them.

'I'm really looking forward to GCU camp,' she said, remembering back to before she went to Congo when she had cleared out the room behind her mother's garage in order to use it for GCU meetings.

'And it will be lovely to be in Scotland again.'

* * *

'Tell me about the girls,' she asked the person in charge, as they waited for them to arrive.

'There are sixty of them, between ten and seventeen years old, and they come from all over the UK.'

'Two weeks is a long time to have sixty girls together,' thought Helen aloud.

Her friend smiled. 'There are twelve leaders and I'm sure there's plenty for us to do here.'

'Two weeks gives us long enough to do quite a lot of Bible study with them,' Helen said, 'and that is such a privilege.'

No sooner were the words spoken than the first group of girls arrived.

'Come and I'll show you to your dorm,' Helen said brightly, remembering back to the day she was first shown into her dormitory when she went away to boarding school. They climbed several flights of stairs before reaching a room in the top floor.

'This bed creaks,' one of the girls laughed, when she sat down on it.

'Boarding school beds are made with creaks in them,' joked Helen. 'They are put in specially so that teachers and camp leaders can hear when girls get out of bed during the night for midnight feasts!'

'What a view!' said one of the other girls. 'It's beautiful!'

They all gathered round the little window.

'Look!' said the mischief of the group. 'We could get out of the window and crawl down the roof. It's just a gentle slope and it would be quite safe.'

Helen coughed to remind them she was there.

'That's why we have squeaks in the beds!' she laughed and then left them to unpack.

* * *

Camp was a huge amount of fun. The girls visited Elgin, where they saw its ancient ruined cathedral and ate its rather nice ice cream. They played tennis on the school tennis courts and paddled in the River Spey. The water was bitterly cold despite it being the middle of summer. The younger girls rolled down the slope in front of the school until their heads spun. Despite the squeaky beds, they even managed to have some midnight feasts ... which the camp leaders *might* not have known about.

* * *

'We would very much like you to become involved in GCU again now that you are settled back here in

Britain,' Helen had been told before the camp.

Her time at Aberlour made her realise just how much she wanted to teach a group of girls from the Bible week after week after week. Camp helped Helen to know that this was one thing God wanted her to do, and the Lord used that camp in another wonderful way too.

'Where is your home going to be?' one of the leaders asked her.

Pat Morton, also a doctor, lived with her mother near Belfast. She had brought a group of girls over the Irish Sea to the Aberlour camp.

'I don't really know,' said Helen. 'I'm rather like a snail at the moment. Because I carry all I need with me, my home is wherever I am. I don't have a permanent address.'

'Mother and I have talked this over,' Pat told her friend. 'We have plenty of space and we would like you to feel at home in our home. You can use it as a base if the Lord sends you travelling and when you stop travelling you can make your home with us.'

Helen was thrilled with the kindness of the offer. As she thought it over, a verse from the Bible came into her mind.

'Jesus said, "Everyone who has left houses or brothers or sisters or father or mother or children or fields for my sake will receive a hundred times as much and will inherit eternal life' (Matthew 19:29).

She had given up the idea of marriage, a family and a home of her own to serve the Lord in Africa. Now God was giving her a home with her friend Pat Morton and Pat's mother in Northern Ireland.

* * *

The weather forecast in early January 1978 was not good. Helen knew to leave plenty of time for her long drive from the south coast of England to Durham, where she was to speak at an evening meeting.

'It's starting to snow,' she noted, as she drove north.

'I hope it clears before I drive back tomorrow.'

The weather grew worse and Helen noticed that the gauge showed that the car was low in petrol.

'Oh,' she thought, 'that is a bother.'

Her thoughts turned into prayer.

'Lord, you know that I need to get to London tomorrow and that I don't have much money for petrol. Please will you arrange that I'm given cash for my travelling expenses rather than a cheque in Durham. You know that I can't use a cheque written out to me to buy petrol.'

Driving on, she left the petrol to the Lord and concentrated on what she was going to say to the students.

'This is for your expenses,' a young woman told her at the end of the meeting, as she handed her an envelope.

Smiling, Helen thanked her and put the envelope in her bag. When she was shown to her room a short time later, she opened the envelope and discovered she'd been given a book-token!

The following morning, having bought petrol with every penny she had – and it was not very much – she drove towards London, where she was staying with friends overnight before continuing on her journey.

'You know what you are doing, Lord,' Helen prayed, as she drove with the petrol gauge on red. So it was with a big thank-you to her heavenly Father that she parked the car outside her friend's house with only about a teaspoonful of petrol left in the tank.

'Helen,' her host said, 'would you be willing to speak to a meeting this evening? There will be about 300 people there, good honest working men and women.'

Looking round at the people that night Helen might have thought that any expenses they would give her would not be very much, for they were not well-off.

'We'd like to give you the offering,' a man told her when the meeting was over, and he emptied the entire offering box into her handbag!

'Goodness me,' thought Helen, when she lifted up her bag. 'It's heavy!'

There were hardly any notes in the offering, and Helen had to pay for her petrol the next day by counting out a very large number of coins. But God had answered her prayer and given her more than enough to buy petrol to get her back to the south coast of England.

* * *

The meetings Helen was asked to speak at were not always for adults. It was during a time of power strikes in Northern Ireland that she was invited to a school near her new home.

'What do you know about the school?' she asked her friend Pat.

'It's a splendid place,' was the reply. 'About 200 severely physically disabled children are taught there. What have you been asked to speak about?'

Helen looked serious. 'They've asked me to speak about the challenge of being a missionary. I'm going to have to think hard about how to do that.'

'Yes, you will,' Pat agreed. 'But the Lord wants Christian disabled children to be missionaries for him too.'

After a great deal of thought Helen had her talk ready. She had some other things ready too.

'Good morning, boys and girls,' she said to 200 shining faces. 'I've brought some interesting things to show you.'

The children looked at what she produced: one old damaged oil lantern with its glass painted black and one very shiny new one with sparkling clean glass.

'There have been power cuts in Belfast recently,' she reminded them, 'and we've all been using candles and torches and lanterns to help us to see. Let me tell you about these two oil lanterns.'

Helen struck a match and lit the wick in the old damaged lantern. Then she struck another match and lit the wick in the shiny new lantern. The children watched what she was doing with eyes wide open.

'Each of us is like one of these lanterns,' Helen explained to her audience, who sat as quiet as could be to hear what she was saying. 'If we invite Jesus, who is the Light of the World, into our hearts we become shining lights for him because he shines through us.'

'Please put the lights out,' she asked a teacher.

As soon as the lights went out the children could see a difference between the two lanterns. The new one was shining brightly and the old one didn't give out any light at all through its blackened windows!

'Now watch this,' Helen said, taking the clean glass out of the new lantern and putting it in the damaged one, and taking the black glass out of the old lantern and putting it in the new one. 'Which one is shining more brightly now?' she asked the children.

They hadn't seen the switch-over because the lights were out.

'Please put the lights on again,' Helen said.

What a surprise the boys and girls had when they

realised that the lantern that shone out brightly was the old damaged one.

Helen looked round at the children in front of her. Many of them couldn't walk, some couldn't feed themselves, and others couldn't sit up properly without support.

'You know, girls and boys, it doesn't really matter what the outside of the lantern is like so long as the light is inside, the lantern is filled with oil and the glass is polished. If your heart is filled with the love of God, you can shine for him wherever he puts you, even if some people think that your body is battered and damaged. You can be of more use as missionaries where you live than those who have perfect bodies but who don't have the light of Jesus shining from their hearts through clean lives.'

Many of those children went home from school that day having learned one of the most important lessons of their young lives. You don't have to have a perfect body to be special to your Heavenly Father, and you don't have to be able to run and jump and skip and dance in order to be a missionary for the Lord Jesus Christ.

* * *

It was when Helen was visiting Australia that she met a girl who needed her help. She had just spoken to a large meeting about giving up the things that get between us and serving the Lord.

'If you are willing to give up the thing in your life that is getting between you and Jesus,' she said at the end, 'please come forward as we sing the last song and surrender that thing to him.'

A few came forward, and a girl of about thirteen looked as though she was going to join them but changed her mind and left with two friends.

'Would it help to talk to me?' Helen asked a woman whom she saw was weeping quietly. When the woman spoke it was obvious that she was American.

'We have two daughters, one aged thirteen and the other fifteen,' she began. 'We moved here as missionaries last year. Our older daughter settled down well, but the younger one is tearing the family apart. She hasn't settled down at all and she's being really awful. We don't know what to do to help her.' She stopped, blew her nose, and went on. 'Back home in America we lived on Grandma's farm and she had a horse there.'

The woman stopped speaking as two of the three girls Helen had noticed earlier arrived at the end of the row of seats.

'Good evening!' Helen said, smiling at them both.

'Good evening!' one replied.

The other grudgingly said, 'Hi.'

The first girl had a local accent, the second was American.

'You don't belong here, do you?' Helen asked.

'No.'

She tried again. 'It's not easy living in someone else's country, is it?'

'No.'

The awkward conversation carried on for a little while before Helen had to go to speak with other people.

'Was I too young to go out tonight?' a voice - a young American voice - asked Helen, a short time later.

It was the thirteen-year-old.

'No. Did you want to?'

She nodded, and the two knelt down together.

Helen spoke quietly. 'You just tell the Lord Jesus what it is you want to give him.'

There was a silence, and then the girl began to sob.

'My horse!' she burst out, tears streaming down her face.

After they had prayed together, she turned to Helen with a tearful smile.

'My mum and dad aren't half going to be pleased,' she said. 'I've made their lives into a living nightmare.'

'Are you going to change that?' asked Helen.

'Oh yes,' the girl said. 'I just want to help them fulfil their dream to be the missionaries they want to be, to serve God as they've always wanted to.'

* * *

In the UK, Helen was given permission from WEC to work for a year with GCU (Girl Crusaders' Union), going round the country encouraging the groups of girls who gathered weekly to study the Bible. During that year she spoke at 400 meetings and drove 24,000 miles. That was an average of more than one meeting and over 65 miles every single day of the year!

* * *

'I wonder if you have thought about this,' Helen said to a GCU group, as she showed them an envelope with an official government stamp on it.

'The letters O. H. M. S. on this envelope shows us that this letter has come from the Queen's government because the letters stand for On Her Majesty's Service.'

Some of the girls looked surprised. They had seen such envelopes often enough, but hadn't realised what the letters stood for.

'If we are Christians,' Helen went on, 'we are O.H.M.S., only we are On His Majesty's Service. We are called to be God's servants. We must be willing to serve him anywhere and at any time, doing whatever job he asks us to do.'

There was some serious discussion that day about what it meant to serve the Lord. During a chat later, an older girl came to Helen with a question. It was about training for missionary service.

'How did you train to be a missionary surgeon?' she enquired. 'Did you have to do special training over and above your medical degree?'

Helen smiled and suggested they sat down.

'Would it surprise you if I told you that I never did train to be a surgeon?'

It certainly did surprise the girl!

'What happened was this...' and as she spoke, Helen's eyes took on a faraway look because the question had taken her right back to Nebobongo.

'I trained to be a physician, not a surgeon. I did no surgery at all during my medical training. I didn't want to. The truth is that the thought of doing surgery almost turned my stomach! One day a woman was brought into the hospital at Nebobongo. She was dangerously ill and surgery was the only possible means of saving her life, and even that was unlikely.'

The girl was listening with great interest.

'There was no surgeon in Nebobongo at that time,' went on Helen. 'I had one white colleague there with me, a nurse. "You're going to have to operate," she told me. "No! I can't!" I protested. "You can and you will!" she insisted. "If you don't, this poor woman will certainly die." I had no choice. I scrubbed up, put on a gown and mask and did what I could.'

'How did you know what to do?' the girl asked. Helen looked a little ashamed. 'I'm afraid the nurse had my book on surgery and she held it open where

I could see it, turning the pages as we went along.'

By now a little group of girls had gathered to hear the story.

'Did the woman survive?' asked one of them.

'She survived the surgery,' Helen admitted. 'But a week later she died of a massive infection. I vowed that I'd never operate again. That was going to be my first and last operation.'

'But it wasn't, was it?' asked a girl who knew a bit about the missionary's story.

'Very soon afterwards,' went on Helen, 'another woman came in with more or less the same problem and she too needed an emergency operation. I had absolutely no choice or I would have had to watch that woman die too. So I operated on her and discovered that I knew what to do. She survived and made a good recovery. That was the beginning of my surgical career.'

Turning to the girl who had asked the question, she smiled broadly.

'If you feel that God is calling you to be a missionary surgeon, I suggest that you do a full training and gain plenty of experience before you go!'

On His Majesty's Service

'What a year it has been!' said Helen, when her time of travelling with GCU was over. 'That was a marathon and a wonderful one.'

Pat smiled. 'It's also a marathon writing job that WEC has given you to do.'

Helen looked up from the pile of papers that surrounded her.

'Yes,' she agreed. 'Being asked to write four books for the Mission is quite a challenge. However, the first one is done. There are only three more to go.'

By then Helen was well known as an author. She had written her story in two parts. The first, from childhood until the rebellion in Congo is called **Give me this Mountain**. And the second which is about her years at Nyankunde, is called **He gave us a valley**. The four she was asked to write by WEC were on faith, holiness, sacrifice and fellowship. Over the next few years, when Helen wasn't travelling she was at her desk researching and writing these books - as well as a history of GCU.

* * *

'I have never met anyone who can get through as much work as you can,' someone said to Helen during an American tour in 1983. 'How many meetings are you speaking at while you are here?'

'I think there are over a hundred during my six week stay in the States,' Helen admitted.

'How on earth do you find something different to say at every meeting,' she was asked.

'I don't, and I don't need to. Someone hearing me on the east coast of America isn't likely to turn up on the west coast four weeks later.'

* * *

Helen thought through her talks very carefully, often using visual aids to help people remember what she had to say. On that particular American tour it was figures that were particularly on her mind.

'You must understand the need to spread the good news that Jesus is the Saviour,' she told many groups of people, especially young people. 'Listen to this. In the world today there are:

- over ten hundred million young people who need to hear about Jesus;
- nine hundred million Muslims who haven't heard the gospel;
- eight hundred million atheists who don't believe in God;
- seven hundred million Roman Catholics who need to be pointed to the Lord;
- six hundred million Hindus who trust in thousands of idols;

- five hundred million Buddhists who know nothing of the power of God;
- four hundred million Protestants who should know the truth, but who often don't live Christian lives;
- three hundred million others like those who dabble in black magic;
- two hundred million born-again Christians who don't always realise they must be missionaries.'

By then Helen's listeners were trying to work out what the 'one' would be. Holding a large '1' up where everyone could see it, she asked, 'Are you the ONE to whom God is speaking today? Is he challenging YOU to be a missionary?'

* * *

Many people who heard Helen's talks on mission had questions they wanted her to answer. Some were very honest in their concerns.

'I'd love to serve the Lord overseas,' one young man said. 'But I sometimes find it really difficult understanding people from other countries. Their lives are so different from ours. You seem to get on so well with the African people you probably don't even understand my problem.'

Helen shook her head. 'Oh yes, I do,' she said. 'For example, Africans take life slowly. They're not nearly as worried as we are about time. That can be really nice and relaxing if you are on holiday. But it isn't if you want to get things done. It was especially difficult for me because I'm one of life's quick people.'

'So how did you cope with that?'

'Sometimes I didn't,' admitted Helen. 'I can remember times when I'd say that we'd do an operation at 2 pm. I'd be there all ready to go ahead and nothing whatever would happen for the next hour and a half. I've seen people die because of that. There were times when that made me very angry and occasionally I spoke sharply to people who kept me waiting.'

The young man bristled. 'So would I,' he said. 'Quite right too!'

'No,' Helen told him. 'It's not right to lose patience with the people you work with. There were times when I had to be told off for that. Pastor Ndugu spoke to me very firmly about it several times. There was even one terrible occasion when I actually raised my hand to an African. I had to apologise to the whole church when I did that. Yet these dear people forgave me and continued to work with me.'

'Pastor Ndugu had no right to do that!' the lad replied. 'You were in charge. You were the missionary doctor.'

Helen looked at him and shook her head. 'How wrong you are. Missionaries are servants of the people they go to, not their masters. I suggest that you abandon any thoughts of being a missionary until you have that worked out in your mind and heart.'

A group of students who overheard that conversation then came to speak to Helen. All were interested in mission as it was a missionary conference they were attending.

'You did get on with the Africans most of the time, didn't you?' one asked.

'Yes,' she assured them. 'The Zairians are very easy to get on with. They are warm and very loving people.'

'I liked what you said about John Mangadima,' commented a girl. 'You two seemed to work so well together that I'm sure there were never any disagreements between you.'

Helen's mind whizzed back through the years to when she worked with John, first at Ibambi, then Nebobongo, and then at Nyankunde.

'Let me tell you a little bit about John,' she said. 'His dream was to be a doctor but he could only go up to primary seven at school. After school he went to a state hospital and asked if they would train him to be a doctor. The people there laughed at him and offered him a job as a ward orderly. So he cleaned the wards, helped people with toileting and things like that. It was then he became a Christian. Not long afterwards he was given the job of carrying a bag for a doctor visiting a leprosy camp. One of the patients didn't do what he was told to do and the doctor slapped him. John stepped between the doctor and the patient. "Sir," he said, "you do not strike a man like that." The doctor then struck John so hard that he fell to the ground. John Mangadima rose to his feet, turned the other side of his face to the doctor, and was slapped so hard that once again he landed on the ground. Struggling to his feet, John looked that white doctor in the eye and said, "My Master is the Lord Jesus Christ, Sir, not you." He was dismissed from his job there and then.'

'Brave guy!' said the girl, who had asked the question.

'Yes, indeed,' Helen agreed. 'Not long afterwards John arrived at my door. He would be about seventeen years old. After we had spoken for a minute or two, he said to me, "You're a Christian, aren't you?" I said that I was. "You're a doctor, aren't you?" I said that I was. "Well,' said John Mangadima, "I want to be a doctor too. Will you make me into one?"

Everyone around Helen was smiling at the thought of the young man's boldness.

'And you know the rest of the story, how John eventually became Assistant Director of the hospital at Nebobongo. But what I've told you about him shows how fair and how firm he was. John Mangadima would not put up with anything he thought was unfair, especially if it was unfair against one of his own people. European and African ideas of fairness can be different and there were times when John and I disagreed. It didn't matter to him that I was the missionary doctor. If he thought I was doing wrong or being unfair, he was very quick to tell me. I love John Mangadima from the bottom of my heart, but there were times when we nearly drove each other mad!'

A student, who until then had said nothing, touched Helen's arm.

'Thank you so much for telling us that,' he said. 'It's helpful to remember that even if we do go to the mission field everything won't always be wonderful there.'

* * *

In 1988 a letter arrived on Helen's doormat that made her heart race.

'As you know I've made videos for missionary societies all over the world,' wrote Crawford Telfer. 'Would you consider going back to Zaire with me to make a video about mission?'

It was fifteen years since Helen had said her goodbyes in Zaire, and now she had the opportunity to go back! But did she really want to go? So many of those she had loved had died. Things would be so different. Would it work? Had she forgotten all her Swahili? Was it right to go back after all that time? As soon as Helen felt sure that was what God wanted her to do, she said 'yes' and started serious planning.

Laden with cameras and all the other things needed to make a film, a Mission Aviation Fellowship plane landed in Nyankunde where a thousand people burst into song. Boys beat drums in time to the singing until their wrists must have ached.

'Up you go!' Helen was told, as she was helped on to a lorry with an armchair on top.

Enthroned on the chair, their old friend was driven slowly round the whole village. Up and down the paths she was taken, through lines of cheering singing people. For a week the film crew followed Helen around, taking hour after hour of film.

'I'd like a shot of you at the top of that hill,' Crawford told her.

Helen looked up the hill, so familiar from all those years ago. But when they reached the top she admitted that she'd never been up there before.

The film crew looked staggered. 'Why not?' one of them asked.

Helen looked just a little embarrassed and then admitted that she'd never had the time!

From Nyankunde they flew, a week later, to Nebobongo. The film crew went ahead of Helen in order to record her arrival. Dressed in a pink skirt, with her jacket hanging over her arm, Helen climbed out of the Mission Aviation Fellowship plane on the Nebo airstrip. As she raised her arms to wave to her friends her jacket flew like a flag of greeting. Singing erupted from hearts fit to burst. Recognising one person after another, Helen threw her arms around her old friends. Then John Mangadima came forward, his eyes brimming with tears, and hugged Helen close to his heart. Mama Luka (her African name) was home.

She was to go home to Nebobongo one more time after that, in 2004, to open a new surgical unit in the hospital. When the unit's African name is translated into English it is The Surgical Centre of Mama Luka. Older women in Africa are known as mamas, Helen included. Luke, who wrote the gospel of Luke in the Bible, was a doctor. That's why her African friends joined the two together and called their doctor Mama Luka.

One of the great thrills of that visit was that Helen and Pat, who by then had retired and was able to travel with her, were taken to visit the village where John Mangadima was born.

'I can't believe my eyes!' Helen gasped, when she looked around it. 'A hospital!'

'The people had no medical care so I build this little hospital,' John explained.

Pat, who had been a hospital doctor, was most interested. 'What are you able to do here?' she asked.

'We have medical, surgical and maternity wards,' was the reply.

'And a school!' exclaimed Helen, unable to contain her excitement.

John nodded. 'There was a primary school with hundreds of pupils, but no secondary school for them to go to. I built this secondary school and there are five teachers here now.'

'How many children?' enquired Pat.

'There are sixty secondary pupils,' she was told.

Helen was totally overwhelmed. John had come to her fifty-four years ago asking to be trained as a doctor and Helen had taught him all she knew. But her pupil had watched what else she did and had learned the need for schools and good hospital facilities and had built both in his own home village.

* * *

Since making her home in Northern Ireland, Helen and her friend Pat Morton have taken a GCU class on Sunday afternoons. While studying the Bible takes up the main part of the meeting, there is also time for talking together. From time to time the girls ask Helen about her missionary experiences.

'Please will you tell us my favourite story of when you were in Nebobongo,' a GCU girl asked one day.

'What story is that?' enquired Helen, knowing very well what story it was.

'About little orphan Ruth,' was the answer she expected and the answer she received.

Smiling at the memory of what happened, Helen settled down to tell the story. The girls, who knew it so well that they could have told it themselves, sat back to enjoy it.

'Not long after I went to Nebobongo I was called out during the night to the maternity unit,' she began. 'A mother was having trouble delivering her baby. Despite everything we did to help her that poor woman died and we were left with a tiny premature baby to look after, as well as the baby's two-year-old sister. "We'll have to keep this little baby warm," I told the nurse who was with me. It gets very cold during the night in Africa and I knew that if the baby cooled down he would die. The nurse rushed to get the box we used for premature babies. We used to wrap them in cotton wool and then put them in the box with a hot water bottle on either side to keep them cosy. But a few minutes later the nurse came back looking very worried. "What's wrong?" I asked her. "I was filling up the hot water bottle when it burst!" she exclaimed. "And it was the very last one we have." It was so important to keep that little baby warm that the nurse had to cuddle him most of the night.'

The girls were sitting listening, so absorbed in the story that it was as though they had never heard it before!

The following day I went to have prayers with the orphan children at lunchtime,' continued Helen. 'I used to do that every day. I gave them some things to pray for and then told them about the little baby and the two-year-old who was crying because her mummy had died. Some of the children prayed for the baby and his sister. Ruth, who was ten years old, began to pray. "God," she said, "please send a hot water bottle so that this little baby doesn't die. And, God, it will be no use sending it tomorrow because we need it today. And, God, while you're at it, will you send a dolly for the baby's sister who is crying because her mummy has died." I gulped when Ruth prayed that prayer and I didn't even say 'amen' because I didn't think the Lord could do that.'

The girls smiled at each other. They liked it when Helen was honest enough to admit that there were things she found hard to believe.

'That afternoon someone came into the ward I was in. "A truck has just delivered a parcel for you and driven off straight away." 'Well!' said Helen. 'I'd never had a parcel delivered in all the time I'd been in the Congo! I looked at it, all wrapped up in brown paper, with English postage stamps on the corner and strong string holding it together. As I just knew I couldn't open it alone I called the orphan children over to help me. We untied the string, unwrapped the paper and opened the cardboard box. The children's eyes were like saucers. They'd never seen a parcel unwrapped before! We took out knitted baby cardigans, soap and bandages. Then, as I pushed my hand down further, I felt the cold rubber of a hot water bottle! My heart nearly burst. When I pulled it out of the box the children cheered. Ruth, when she saw the bottle, jumped to her feet. "If God sent the hot water bottle, he'll have sent the dolly too!" she yelled, and yanked the rest of the stuff out of the parcel. There, at the bottom, was what she was sure would be there. Just imagine the excitement when Ruth pulled the dolly out of the parcel! There was such a cheer! I wanted to cheer too but I was in tears of joy and amazement at God's goodness.'

There was quietness for a moment or two as the girls let the story settle into their minds and hearts. Then one of them broke the silence.

'Do you know what I especially love about that story?' she asked.

Helen shook her head.

'I love the fact that the parcel took months to get from England to Nebobongo but God had made sure that the person who packed it put just the right things in, and that it came on the very day it was needed.'

'God knows all things,' Helen told the girls. 'He knew when I was your age that one day I'd go to Africa. He knew I'd be in Ibambi, Nebobongo and Nyankunde. God knew what would happen during the rebellion and he allowed it all for his own good reasons that I don't fully understand. He knew that Pat and I would be running this GCU class and that you would all be here today. And he knows what your futures are too. Perhaps he knows that some of you will go abroad to be missionaries for him in foreign places. But even if you stay here at home, he has a job for you to do. It's the same job, because Christians should be missionaries wherever they are.'

That was Helen's message following her return from Africa. For over thirty years she has criss-crossed the world telling Christians – especially young Christians – that they should be missionaries. Sometimes she speaks to one person at a time, on other occasions to many thousands gathered together. That's still what she is saying today: if you are God's child, you are On His Majesty's Service and you too are called to be a missionary.

Thinking Further Topics

The following pages will help you to think about the different issues raised in the book.

Chapter 1

Piggy in the Middle

How did Freda, the nursemaid, gain the respect of Helen and her brother and sisters?

While learning in Sunday School about the country of India, Helen tried to imagine what it must feel like not to have heard about God. She felt challenged to become a missionary some day. Have missionary stories ever given you the desire to do the same?

What is every Christian called to do? Read Matthew 28:19.

Helen tried very hard to be liked. Do you sometimes pretend to be different from who you really are in order to be popular? Is that a good thing to do?

Chapter 2

The Day Helen didn't meet Hitler

Helen believed black people are just the same inside as white people. Why is there so much racism today? How do you feel about those of a different race or religion?

Helen told lies about meeting Adolf Hitler in order to be popular with her friends. Do you ever tell lies and why? Read Deuteronomy 5:20.

When Helen's father was given an important job during the war, Helen was keen to boast about it to her friends. However, her father persuaded her otherwise, because he said that everyone involved in the war effort is important.

Do you ever boast to your friends about something that you have or do? What does the Bible say about boasting? Read 2 Corinthians 10:17.

Chapter 3

Battles inside and out

After Helen's confirmation she felt really bad if she told a lie. It is very easy to get into a habit of lying. Why is being truthful important?

What was it that gave Helen a broken heart? What saddens God's heart? Read Luke 13:34.

Many people ask the question, Why do wars and famines and earthquakes happen? What does the Bible have to say? Read Matthew 24:3-8.

After Helen asked God to forgive her sins she felt she had to do something - what did she do? Have you ever felt the same way?

Chapter 4

Medical student

What Scripture verse spoke right into Helen's heart? Helen knew this was the moment she found Jesus as her Saviour. Can you recall a particular verse in the Bible which spoke very clearly to you?

Do you know in your heart that you are a Christian? If not, what should you do?

One day Helen was asked lots of questions by a man on the train about her new-found faith. We should never be embarrassed about our faith. Read 2 Timothy 1:8.

How can we know what God wants us to do with our lives? Read Proverbs 3:5.

Chapter 5

Called to the Congo

What was the greatest lesson that Helen learned at missionary training college?

In the Garden of Gethsemane, Jesus fell with his face to the ground and prayed, 'My Father, if it is possible, may this cup be taken from me. Yet not as I will, but as you will' (Matthew 26:39). Jesus longed to do the will of his Father alone, no matter what the cost would be.

Helen soon became tired and stressed while working at the hospital in the Congo. She turned away a blind lady who had waited all morning for someone to take her to the clinic. What would Jesus have done? Read Luke 18:35-43.

God blessed the people in Nebobongo and filled them with the joy of the Lord. How did Helen experience the same joy?

Chapter 6

Rebellion!

What helped Helen most during the early days of civil unrest? Do you have someone to turn to when things go wrong in life?

What words of Dr Scroggie did Helen remember during the difficult time of rebellion? Do you have wise words or Scripture verses you can hold on to during difficulties?

What does the Bible say about suffering for our faith? Read John 16:33.

God loves us so much that he gave his own Son on the Cross. Because he loves, he suffered, giving us an example to follow (1 Peter 2:21).

Chapter 7

'You build, I teach'

What was the reaction of the students when Helen asked them to become workmen in order to build dormitories and a nursing school? How would you have reacted?

Helen's prayer was that graduates would not only go out medically trained, but would take the good news of Jesus Christ with them. Read Galatians 2:2.

God calls us not only to be missionaries, but to share our faith in whatever job we find ourselves. Read 2 Timothy 4:2 and 1 Peter 3:15.

Chapter 8

The Miracle of Nyankunde

Helen's day began at 5 am when she had her quiet time with God. Are you willing to get up early to spend time with God before the day begins?

Jesus set the example for us concerning our quiet time. Read Mark 1:35.

God provided a roofer just at the right time to complete the building work on the classroom block and money came from the education authority just when it was needed. He has promised to provide all of our needs. Read Philippians 4:19.

Nyelongo was concerned that money would be taken from his pay because his baby was in hospital. However, this was not the case and that day he and his wife asked the Lord Jesus to be their Saviour. God calls people to himself in so many different ways and circumstances.

Chapter 9

Passport Please

GCU camp helped Helen in two ways - she felt that teaching at camp was something God wanted her to do and she was offered a base in the home of Pat Morton.

Jesus said, 'Everyone who has left houses or brothers or sisters or father or mother or children or fields for my sake will receive a hundred times as much and will inherit eternal life' (Matthew 19:29).

What did the physically disabled children learn from the story Helen told about the two lanterns? Read Matthew 5:16.

What does it mean to be On His Majesty's Service?

Chapter 10

On His Majesty's Service

So many people have never heard about Jesus Christ and salvation. How are they going to hear?

Helen said to one person asking about missionary work, 'Missionaries are servants of the people they go to, not their masters.'

What does the name 'Mama Luka' mean? What did Luke do for a living? Read Colossians 4:14.

Did the story about orphaned Ruth's prayer encourage you to have a child-like trust that God will answer prayer?

'Do not be anxious about anything, but in everything, by prayer and petition, with thanksgiving, present your requests to God' (Philippians 4:6).

Time Line
Helen Roseveare

1925   Helen Roseveare was born.

1928   Penicillin discovered by Alexander Fleming.

1931   Empire State building completed.

1934   The introduction of 'apartheid' in South Africa.

1935   Germany issued the anti-Jewish Nuremberg Laws.

1936   Nazi Olympics held in Berlin.

1938   The IRA carried out the first bombings in Britain.

1939   World War Two began.

1940   Germany bombed England.
Winston Churchill became Prime Minister.

1941   Japanese attacked Pearl Harbour.

1944   D-Day.
Helen Roseveare left school and began her study of medicine at Cambridge. It was there she became a Christian.

1948   The State of Israel founded.

1951   Helen Roseveare was missionary candidate at WEC headquarters.

1952   Princess Elizabeth became Queen.

1960   The Belgian Congo achieved independence.

1964   Helen Roseveare was taken prisoner by rebel forces and remained a prisoner for five months during the civil war.

1966   Joseph Mobutu changed the Congo's official name to Zaire.
Helen Roseveare returned to the Congo to

assist in the rebuilding of the nation. She helped establish a new medical school.

1969	Neil Armstrong became the first man on the moon.
1973	UK joined the EEC.
1973	Helen Roseveare returned to the United Kingdom.
1976	She spoke at a missionary conference in America.
1979	Margaret Thatcher became first woman Prime Minister of Great Britain.
1988	Helen Roseveare returned to Nebobongo to make a video for missionary societies.
1989	Berlin Wall came down. Helen Roseveare's life of service was portrayed in the film *Mama Luka Comes Home*.
1991	Collapse of the Soviet Union.
1993	World Trade Center bombed.
1994	Rwandan genocide began. Channel Tunnel opened.
1997	Hong Kong returned to China.
2004	Helen Roseveare returned to Nebobongo to open a new surgical unit.
2007	Helen continues to have strong links with the Cambridge Inter-Collegiate Christian Union and was designated as the 'CICCU missionary' during the 1950s and 1960s. Since her return from Africa in 1973, she has had a worldwide ministry in speaking and writing. Three of her books are: He gave me this Mountain (1966), He gave us a Valley (1977) and Digging Ditches (2005). She was a speaker at Urbana three times and now lives in Northern Ireland.

CHRISTIAN FOCUS PUBLICATIONS

Christian Focus | Christian Heritage | CF4K | Mentor

Christian Focus Publications publishes books for adults and children under its four main imprints: Christian Focus, Christian Heritage, CF4K and Mentor. Our books reflect that God's word is reliable and Jesus is the way to know him, and live for ever with him.

Our children's publication list includes a Sunday school curriculum that covers pre-school to early teens; puzzle and activity books. We also publish personal and family devotional titles, biographies and inspirational stories that children will love.

If you are looking for quality Bible teaching for children then we have an excellent range of Bible story and age specific theological books.

From pre-school to teenage fiction, we have it covered!

Find us at our web page:
www.christianfocus.com

CF4·K
*Because you're never
too young to know Jesus*